Advance Praise for Souls' ...

Souls' Rescue offers a fresh new voice to lesbian fiction. The author has written a well-crafted story with realistic scenes of firefighting and rescue work. The characters are believable and struggle with life-altering challenges. But the most harrowing challenge of all is the one that scares them the most—falling in love again. *Souls' Rescue* is a promising debut for Pat Cronin.

~ **Chris Paynter**, author
Playing for First and *Come Back to Me*

This novel centers on the lives of two strangers whose destinies bring them together amidst the devastation of one thoughtless act. A story very much grounded in human emotions, human frailties and strengths along with the raw vulnerabilities that ultimately make us all seek the comfort of another soul.

~ **Verda Foster**
Goldie Award winning co-editor for *Blue Collar Lesbian Erotica*
Goldie Award finalist author of *The Gift*

Firefighting is a necessary, exciting, and always dangerous vocation. Author Pat Cronin comes from a family of firefighters, and it's evident throughout Souls Rescue. She takes the reader into the gritty, smoke-filled, ferocious heat of precarious rescues, including a flashback to 9-11, and with deft descriptions, puts us right there in the mix. Readers who like action will thoroughly enjoy this story, and those who like romance will connect to the ups and downs of the unlikely pairing that Cronin so skillfully presents. Souls Rescue will heat your skin and warm your heart.

~ **Nann Dunne**, author, editor, and publisher of Just About Write, www.JustAboutWrite.com

Souls' Rescue

Pat Cronin

Yellow Rose Books

Port Arthur, Texas

ISBN 978-1-935053-30-9
1-935053-30-2

First Printing 2010

9 8 7 6 5 4 3 2 1

Cover design by Donna Pawlowski

Published by:

Regal Crest Enterprises, LLC
4700 Highway 365, Suite A, PMB 210
Port Arthur, Texas 77642

Find us on the World Wide Web at
http://www.regalcrest.biz

Printed in the United States of America

Acknowledgments

I want to first thank my dear friend and editor, Lori L. Lake. She's been my mentor in this writing journey and it is because of her patience and teaching that I've gotten to this level.

Thanks to J Robin Whitley for her edits and comments.

A great big gigantic thanks to my bestest friend, Verda Foster, for her help on this novel and all it's million incarnations. You can't ask for a better friend.

THANKS TO :

Chris Paynter, Nann "Nanna" Dunne, my sis Marie, Mary H, Jessie Chandler and Lynn Glover for their quick feedback and wonderful comments.

My brother-in-law, James, for letting me kill him and then sue him.
Drinks are on me!

My publisher and friend, Cathy LeNoir for taking a chance on me. You rock!

Donna P for the awesome cover.

My mom and granny for the endless card games!

And a very special thanks to my wife, Sandra. *Ik hou van jou, liefje. Voor altijd!*

To the memory of my dad, George, and my granddad, Frank. The two most important men in my life.

Chapter
One

THE ATRIUM OF the Winchester Building was busier than usual. Talia Stoddard stood in line at the Starbucks, checking her watch to make sure she would be on time. She had her own office as the Associate of Claims for the Winchester Insurance Group.

The morning sun beamed through the glass walls of the atrium and lit the open area with tiny speckles of light. Rainbows floated along the streams of sunshine. Talia wondered if any of the other Monday morning workers ever took time to enjoy the beauty of the sparkling colors.

The line moved and she inched forward. She could hear the first bit of Reba McIntire's "Is There Life Out There." Six months ago she couldn't have imagined herself standing in line at Starbucks and hearing country music. It wouldn't happen back in DC. But Cincinnati was a world away from the nation's capital and she was glad for it.

Her cell phone rang, announcing that her best friend and co-worker Jacob Meier was calling. She waited for her Bluetooth to activate. " 'Morning, Jacob."

"Hi darlin'. Are you here yet?"

"Nope. I'll be up in about ten or fifteen minutes, I guess. Why? Is there something urgent you need?"

"Yes. I'm dying as we speak. I need my cappuccino. Besides, you have to tell me what you think of that new yummy barista."

"I can see him from where I am. Why?"

"Because he's going out with me next week."

Talia smiled. "You are such a whore-dog."

"Yes, and proud of it."

"Of course you are. I'll be in the office in a bit, and you can tell me all about him."

"Good. Now hurry up. I need my caffeine."

"Yes, dear."

Talia got their morning order and headed for the elevators, her high heels clicking against the smooth white tiles that somehow never seemed to smudge. She thought that the Winchester Group must spend a pretty penny to keep the building so shiny and spotless.

The regular, enclosed cars were empty, but she waited for the glass elevator. Even though it took forever to actually take off, it felt

more open and a lot less claustrophobic than the others. She could
see her reflection and straightened the collar of her new silk blouse.
Jacob had insisted she buy some new clothes because he was tired of
all the black and navy pantsuits she wore.

They had spent all day Saturday going to every shop in
Cincinnati. She'd spent a lot of money on new shirts and slacks and
Jacob came away with the phone numbers of two very helpful young
men.

The shirt she wore was Jacob's favorite pick. It was light yellow
and even though she wasn't sure it looked good with her dark brown
features, Jacob insisted it highlighted her eyes. Her mother would be
appalled and for that reason alone, Talia bought the shirt.

The elevator car arrived and she stepped in and pressed 10 with
her free hand, glad that no one else was riding with her.

The back of the elevator formed a diamond point, and through
each panel of glass she was treated to a stunning visual of the
upward sweep of Cincinnati's twenty floor architectural wonder, the
Winchester Building. She wasn't all that fond of skyscrapers, but this
was a building that oozed grace and loveliness. She gazed out into
the atrium and took a sip of her cappuccino.

Over the hum of everyday sounds outside the elevator, Talia
heard an explosive crash. A woman screamed. A high pitched engine
shrieked, and her ears hurt from the sound.

As she whirled toward the elevator doors, she was shocked to
see a flash of blue and white careening toward her.

"Oh, my g—"

She didn't have time to say another word or let go of the coffee
before a giant metal monster smashed her backwards. Glass rained
down. The sunlight blinked out. Pressure all around sucked away
the air until every little gasp she made brought in only dust.

Something hot and wet trickled down the front of her, and the
last thought she managed before passing out was to wonder if that
was coffee – or her own blood.

Chapter
Two

KELLY MCCOY SLUNG the air pack over one shoulder and headed for the work bench in the back of the fire house bay. Her footsteps echoed on the concrete as she passed where Ladder 7 and Engine 12 were normally parked. Those crews had responded to a fire call just before her shift started two hours earlier. She was jealous that they were out fighting fire while she was stuck doing busy work and checking air bottles.

"Yo, Kel." Scott Sanderson, a firefighter on her shift and Kelly's best friend, came running over. "Which pack you got?"

She glanced at the number on the strap. "Nineteen. Why?"

"Shit. I'm working on inventory, and I can't find pack twelve."

Kelly was about to respond when alert tones sounded throughout the bay, echoing off the cinder block walls and calling for Engine 14, Rescue 1, to respond to the Winchester Building at 324 Vine Street.

"Damn." Kelly put down the air pack and ran for her gear rack, pushing past Scott to get to her boots, coat and helmet. She was dressed first and leapt into the cab of the rescue unit, grinning at Scott when he climbed in behind her. She was in the forward facing seat, but Scott had to sit in the seat in front of her that faced backward. Knowing riding backward made him car sick, she flashed him a mocking smile.

"I hate you," Scott said.

"No you don't."

"You only dress faster than me because you're shorter."

Kelly reached forward to whap him in the stomach. "I beat you because you're getting old and fat."

"I am not."

Jimmy Mills, their shift lieutenant, chimed in from the officer's seat on the passenger side of the truck's cab. "Yeah, you are. You're the oldest one here, Sanderson."

Scott displayed his middle finger for both of them. "You're only a couple months younger than me, Jimmy."

"I'm still younger."

"Bite me."

Jason Burke launched himself into the driver's seat and tore out of the station with the siren wailing.

Kelly felt a sudden tightening in her gut as they rolled up to the

Winchester Building. The feeling didn't happen often, but Kelly knew it meant the call would be a bad one.

The building's lower floor entrance had been encased in solid glass, which now littered the sidewalk. A truck had left a gaping whole in an otherwise pristine, glass encased entrance. Sharp edges of the window lined the space where a door once stood. Pieces of the metal hung from the remnants of the frame.

"Get in there," Jimmy hollered. "Looks damn bad!"

Kelly grabbed the emergency medical bag and headed into the building, skirting a twisted railing. Glass crunched beneath her boots. She stepped over briefcases and around display racks and paused for a moment to take in the wide array of destruction. She looked back to the hole in the wall and quickly took in the back half of a giant delivery truck, its nose buried inside the bank of elevators.

Bodies littered the scene. She heard a grinding motor and smelled exhaust. Kelly was reminded of a television broadcast about the conflicts in the Middle East. The few people on their feet moved about as though dazed, blood dripping from facial cuts, while others sat on the ground nursing injuries. She counted five lying on the ground not moving at all. She met Scott's eye and he shook his head in amazement before hastening toward his first victim.

Kelly put her bag down next to the first person she came upon. The man was sitting with his legs crossed, leaning against a piece of wood that had probably once belonged to the information desk. His black suit, white shirt and black silk tie reminded her of FBI agent attire. "Sir, are you hurt?"

He didn't say anything—just stared ahead with eyes fixed on something behind Kelly. She did a quick assessment, noting he was breathing and had no obvious injuries. No blood and no reaction when she touched him. She placed a string around his neck with a green tag on the end of it to tell other responders that he had no life-threatening injuries.

She hustled to the next person and repeated her assessment—a roll of clean gauze to staunch blood from a cut on the arm and another green tag applied.

"What the fuck are you doing? We don't have time to be fucking with a small bleeder."

Kelly looked up at Jason Burke. His large frame blocked the outside light. Made more from blubber than bulk, he moved slow and had never been known to be good at his job. He'd driven their engine to the scene and she'd immediately lost track of him. "I'm doing my job. What are you doing?"

"Your job isn't to put band aids on people. Get them tagged and move on."

She got to her feet and glared at him. Burke was a giant pain in her ass and she didn't have time or energy to spare to argue with him. "Bite me."

Kelly maneuvered around him to a young woman lying face-down, far from the wreckage of the truck. From the rag-doll positioning of her body, Kelly thought she must have been hit and thrown the distance. Blood pooled around her head and shoulders. Kelly checked for a pulse and didn't find one. She put a black tag around the woman's wrist that marked her DOA.

Kelly rose to go to the next patient and heard her mic go off. In all the chaos and noise around her, it took a moment for her to hear her lieutenant's voice.

"McCoy. Respond." He sounded irritated.

She turned the volume up and said, "Here."

"Get over to the crash vehicle. Got a confined space rescue I need you for."

"Copy that." Kelly shouldered her bag and picked her way through the debris. At five-four, she was the smallest firefighter at their station, but a guy at Station 20 beat her out for smallest in the department. He hit just five-two, but at 155 pounds, he outweighed her by nearly thirty pounds. Scott was a big lunk of a guy, and most of the other firefighters and paramedics were too broad-shouldered to wriggle into small spaces. Kelly always got called upon instead.

She hurried to cross the mine field of glass and sharp metal, concerned that there were still so many victims down. But just then another group of paramedics and firefighters came flooding through the entrance, and Kelly let out a sigh of relief.

The truck cab had struck and crushed down part of a brick wall that ran like wainscoting between the elevators. The nose was enveloped by brick and glass, and the front wheels were off the ground with part of the undercarriage hung up over the wall, which, at a quick glance, looked to be made of drywall and not real brick. Parts of a glass elevator were mixed in with the myriad of building materials piled all around. It looked to Kelly like the only thing holding the truck at the awkward upward angle was the debris it had dragged through as it crashed.

"What do you need, L-T?"

"Under the truck," Jimmy said, "there's a gap between the front axel and the wood and shit it's sitting on. There's a woman under all that. We heard her when we got the driver out."

"Is he alive?"

"DOA."

Kelly set down the medical bag and removed her turnout gear. The protective clothing would be too bulky to maneuver in. "Where do you want me to enter?"

"Here." Jimmy got down on his haunches and showed her an

opening about a foot wide beneath the roof of the cab. "You're the only one small enough to get in there. I can't tell how much more room you'll have farther in. Soon as we get this thing cribbed up you can check it out."

"I'll get my gear." Kelly ran out to the fire engine where they stored the specialized equipment she would need. In less than two minutes, she was back standing next to her lieutenant, waiting to get started.

The other firefighters had already used dozens of wooden blocks to crib the vehicle to stabilize it. The blocks would keep it from falling over while she was underneath. Somebody got the truck's engine turned off, and for a moment silence took hold as diesel exhaust wafted in the air. And then someone called out in pain, and Kelly heard sobbing from across the atrium. Paramedics called out to one another, and in the distance, she heard the sound of sirens drawing nearer.

Kelly felt sick to her stomach. "I hope she's still alive."

"I don't," Scott said.

Kelly hadn't noticed him standing behind her and turned toward her friend. "Why not? That's kinda harsh, don't you think?"

"No. She's probably got crush injuries, and it's going to take us a long damn time to get her out. She'll code as soon as we lift the weight off."

"Maybe." Kelly couldn't stop looking at the horror of wreckage in front of her. "I don't know, Scott. A crush injury isn't necessarily a death sentence. We could get an ER doc down here in a few minutes."

"Yeah, maybe we should," Scott said.

The crew working to stabilize the truck reported they were done, and Jimmy called out, "Ready, Munchkin?"

"Always, L-T."

"The debris is loose, but it looks like some of the elevator frame has created a V-shaped cavity." He looked away from the small opening and tapped the top of her helmet. "Get in there and see what you can do."

Kelly tied a rope around her waist. It could be used to pull her out if necessary. Leaving her regular medical bag, she accepted a smaller med-pack and got to her knees beside the hole to peer in. Her helmet flashlight lit the small area of the V-shaped void. The light fell upon a dark-skinned arm, and she nearly jumped when the fingers moved and reached for her like a drowning swimmer.

"She's alive," Kelly said and started into the void.

Glass crackled and shifted underneath as she belly-crawled a few inches at a time, pushing the medical kit ahead of her. Time felt like it slowed. Long, metal pieces with sharp edges scraped along her back and shoulders. She was glad to get through the tight tunnel and into a slightly more open space. She estimated she'd gone about five feet and radioed that back to Jimmy. The void opened enough that she could raise herself up onto her elbows. Now she had about twenty-four inches of headroom and figured she must be under some part of the truck chassis. Her patient was just beyond that, her body under debris, and her head protected by the chassis.

The arm moved again as Kelly got close enough to touch it. She removed her gloves and felt for a pulse. It was there. Steady, but faster than it should be. The skin was cool, and as Kelly expected, her patient was already in shock.

"Hey," Kelly called out. "Can you hear me?"

"Yes," came the weak reply.

"Good. My name's Kelly and I'm here to help you."

"I—I can't move."

"Don't worry. My guys are working to get you out. I'm here to take care of you while they do. What's your name?"

"Talia."

"Okay, Talia." Kelly scooted closer and was able to see Talia's upper body. She was lying on her back with her head tilted to one side. Her long, coal black hair was tangled in debris, and Kelly loosened it. When she did, she was startled to see Talia staring right at her. Soft brown eyes blinked several times and Kelly could almost feel the woman's gaze touch her physically. "Are you in pain?"

"My head hurts." Talia closed her eyes for a moment. When she opened them again, Kelly was sure she recognized something familiar. Did she know her from somewhere?

"I'm going to give you some oxygen and then I'm going to put a collar on your neck, okay?"

"Okay."

Kelly took care to keep from moving Talia's head as she got the oxygen line set up, then slipped the hard, plastic collar around her neck. "It's going to be uncomfortable, but I'm giving you the oxygen so you don't feel like you're suffocating."

"Thanks."

"Sure. I'm going to start an IV in your arm to give you some medicine. It might hurt a little."

"I'm hard to get."

"What?"

"I'm hard to get. They always say my arms are too fat and it's hard to find a vein."

"Well, I don't know who 'they' are, but I'm damn good and...I just got it." She finished up the IV and taped it down. "Now I can give you something for your pain."

"I don't like drugs," Talia said without much strength. "I don't want to be out of it."

"It's a small dose of morphine. Should take the edge off the pain. But I won't give it if you don't want it."

"I don't."

Kelly took Talia's blood pressure and relayed the information back to Jimmy. His voice crackled over the mic, "We're going to start extrication."

"Copy."

"What did he say?" Talia asked.

"Time to get you out of here. There's going to be a lot of noise soon, but don't be worried." Kelly retrieved an emergency blanket from her pack. She unfolded it with difficulty and struggled to place it over Talia's head and exposed arm, then ducked beneath it as well. "It's not much, but it'll keep the dust off us."

"I don't like the dark. I don't like this at all."

Kelly scooted as close as she could and placed her hand near the IV on Talia's arm. "I'm here. Just close your eyes and imagine you're somewhere else for the next few minutes. We'll have you out fast. I promise."

Chapter
Three

THE NOISE WAS deafening and Talia felt like her head would explode. Under the blanket, the paramedic's headlamp cast a bright light she could see through her eyelids, but it was too glaring and made her head hurt. She squeezed her eyes so tightly shut they ached, but she didn't want to open them. The only thing that kept her from screaming was the warm pressure of the woman's hand against her forearm. Her voice had a calming effect, and Talia wished she'd start talking again.

"Will it ever stop?" she asked, trying to be heard above the din.

"Soon," Kelly said just as the equipment stopped. "See. Sorry it was so loud. They're right above us probably trying to cut their way through."

"I really need to get out of here." Talia wanted to move her left arm, but it was pinned by something. So were her legs, and when she breathed, a sharp object poked her in the stomach. "It's too tight in here. You don't—I have to get out." She started to pant, but her breath kept getting caught in her throat. She opened her eyes and it was all she could do to keep from screaming.

"Easy there. You're claustrophobic. Here, see if this helps." Kelly shifted so her headlamp lit the cone of space around them.

Talia could now see her rescuer's face. Very green eyes looked back at her and Talia's stomach did a little flip. Kelly smiled and Talia caught her breath, which made her belly get poked again. "Ouch."

"What's hurting?"

"There's something sharp hitting me when I breathe."

"Let's see." Kelly put on her glove and Talia felt her grope at the debris packed hard against her abdomen. "Ah. I can take care of this." She pulled back. "Better?"

Talia released a breath and didn't feel the sharp poke anymore. "What was it?"

"Very big piece of glass. One more thing moved out of the way for you." Kelly situated herself so the light would continue to illuminate their tiny area. "I need to try to check you for other injuries. Just let me know what hurts, okay?"

"I will." Talia tensed a little as gentle hands felt their way down her body. "My stomach hurts when you touch it. So does my right leg, but I can't feel my left one."

"It's pinned. I can't get to it." Kelly placed a hand on Talia's shoulder. "I can't see the injury to your leg, but we'll take care of it as soon as they get us out of here."

"Us? You're staying?"

"Of course. You think I'm leaving before you get out?" Kelly flashed that charming smile again, and Talia felt her insides warm up. "Not a chance. I'm here for the long haul. Okay?"

"Okay." Talia kept her gaze on Kelly. If she concentrated on her, maybe she could forget that she was in a very small, dark space that felt like it was going to crush her completely. The scene reminded her of the movie *Star Wars* when the heroes were in the garbage crusher and nearly got killed. Was this how it would feel? Unable to move and about to die in a prison of bricks and glass held down by a big truck? It was a truck, right? She remembered it coming at her. The coffee was still in her hands. She'd seen the driver's face—why had he kept coming? Why had he done this?

Her mother hadn't wanted her to move back to Cincinnati. Maybe, for once, she'd been right. Maybe Talia should have stayed in DC with her ex, Megan. Her life had been repressive, but she'd still be alive. A wave of pain washed over her. Her heart rate sped up and breathing got harder. Her leg hurt something fierce. Every muscle in her body was screaming in agony, and the pain level seemed to double, triple. She tried to take a deep breath, and then realized she was going to die. She was sure of it.

"I can't do this. Get me out!"

Warm hands cupped the sides of her face and a soothing voice was there, but Talia couldn't make out what was being said. She was going to die, and it would be slow and painful. How the hell had this happened?

"Jacob. I need Jacob," she cried. "Please. Help me!"

"I'm right here," Kelly's voice was louder now, and Talia realized she was speaking in her ear. Talia could feel Kelly's breath on her skin. "I'm here. We're going to get you out."

"Jacob," Talia sobbed. "He's my best friend. He was waiting for his coffee. You have to tell him I'm okay. Please."

"We will. Just as soon as you're out and safe."

"No. You have to get him now. I don't want to die. I've got to talk to him."

Kelly removed one hand to get the microphone of her radio. "Hey, L-T. Any chance you can find a guy named—"

Talia said, "Jacob Meier. He's a lawyer on the tenth floor."

"—Jacob Meier on the tenth floor. He's a friend of our patient and she really wants to talk to him."

There was a pause before they heard, "I'll get someone on it. We're going to start the cutters up again."

Talia sucked in a deep breath of air and tried to calm herself. She couldn't see Kelly's eyes, but felt them looking into hers. "Thank you."

Kelly's reply was drowned out by the roar of the machinery. She kept her gaze on Kelly and hoped they would find Jacob.

THE NOISE ABOVE them stopped, and Kelly took the reprieve to check Talia's vital signs again. Her blood pressure was low and her pulse was rapid. Kelly had already given her a liter of normal saline and called to Jimmy to send another bag. She knew there had to be internal bleeding and felt frustrated that she couldn't get her patient extricated faster.

"McCoy," Jimmy's voice came over the radio, "I've got the saline coming in with another O2 bottle. ER doc from University Hospital can't get here, and the chopper crew is on a call." He paused. "But we've got that guy you wanted."

"Excellent." Kelly placed her shoulder mic close to Talia's face. "I'll press the mic when you want to talk. Okay?"

"Yeah," Talia's voice was softer, weaker than before. "Jacob? Are you there?"

"Hi, sweetie." Kelly could hear a tremor in the man's voice. "I'm right here. It's going to be fine."

"Don't—don't let my mother bully you. Get Sam back here to do the arrangements."

"What? Honey, what arrangements? Oh, hell no. You're not going to die, Talia Stoddard. You hear me? No way."

"I love you, Jacob." Talia closed her eyes, and for a moment Kelly thought she'd passed out. Her pulse was still there, but faint. There wasn't much time left.

"Talia? Don't you dare—"

Jacob's words were cut off and Jimmy's voice came back on the radio. "McCoy, we've got most of the rubble moved away. There's one thing left to cut and we should be able to get some hands in there. Ready?"

"Yep. Just make it quick."

Kelly heard Jimmy giving orders and the voices of the other firefighters above them. "There's going to be more noise, Talia," she said. No response. Kelly moved closer until the upper part of her body was nearly covering Talia's head. She said, "Just hang in there. Keep talking to me."

"Kelly?"

"Yeah?"

"Is there something leaking in here?"

"No. Why?"

"Because something wet is in my eyes."

Kelly moved away and checked Talia's face with her flashlight. Drops of fresh blood trailed along her cheek. There were no cuts or abrasions on Talia's forehead or face. "Shit," Kelly said. She touched her own left temple and felt the wound.

"What's wrong?"

"Sorry. I have a cut on my head. My dad always said I have a hard head. Guess that's why I didn't notice it."

"My dad says that about my brother. Said that's why he became a Marine. His head's so hard nothing will ever hurt it."

Kelly placed a bandage on her temple and held it in place by wrapping gauze around her head. "Marine? Hope he's not in the Middle East right now."

"He's in Germany. He's already done two tours in the war zone."

"You know, I always wanted a brother, but my dad said I was all the boy he ever needed."

"I'm the only girl, the youngest of three. All my dad ever wanted was a little prissy girl to show off."

"Heh. My dad couldn't have made me prissy if he tried. My ma says I was born with the wrong plumbing."

"Not nice."

"She doesn't mean anything by it. She didn't care if I was a tomboy, as long as I was a good kid."

"Were you?" Talia asked.

"Um, sometimes."

Kelly heard a creaking noise that grew steadily louder. It sounded like something was shifting. Kelly braced for debris to fall around them, but the noise stopped.

Kelly keyed her mic. "Jimmy, what's going on?"

"Don't worry about it. Should be breaking through any minute."

"Copy that. Not much longer, Talia." There was no response, so Kelly moved so her light would be near Talia's face. "You okay? Keep talking to me."

"I'm not going to live through this, am I?"

"Don't talk like that. You heard my lieutenant. They're going to get us out of here."

"Not us," Talia said. "You should let them haul you out. I mean, what can you do for me?"

"I can be by your side until you're safely on your way to the hospital." Kelly saw new tears on Talia's face and didn't hesitate to wipe them away. "Hey, don't cry."

"I don't want to die."

"And it's my job to make sure you don't, so I'm not going anywhere." Kelly smoothed her hand over Talia's forehead and felt a strange flutter in her stomach. "I promise."

"Don't make a promise you can't keep."

"Hush." Kelly brushed hair back from Talia's face and resisted the urge to kiss her.

Talia drew in a ragged breath. "Thought you wanted me to talk."

"Smarty. How about no more talk about dying?"

"I'll try."

"There is no try. Only do or do not," Kelly did her best Yoda impression.

"You like *Star Wars*, too?"

"You mean there are people who don't?"

"My mother would never dream of seeing a nonsense movie like that. It would be a waste of her time."

"She doesn't go to the movies?"

"Never. Which is weird, because my dad loves movies. Probably why they're divorced."

"Could be."

"Do your parents go to the movies?" Talia asked.

"They used to go all the time. But my dad died in 2001. "

"Oh, sorry."

Kelly felt tears threaten. Whenever she talked about her dad, that happened, but she forced them back. "It's okay. He was a great dad. Used to take me for rides on the fire truck, let me run around the firehouse like it was my second home. I had more uncles than any other kid I knew, because the other guys were like our family. Still are."

"Wow. What a wonderful childhood that must have been. I always wanted to see a fire truck up close. Well, when I was a kid."

"That can be arranged."

"Really? I mean, I don't want to sound like a nerd or anything."

"Of course you're a nerd," Kelly said. "You like *Star Wars*. That makes you a nerd. And I'll take you on a tour of the station when you're out of the hospital."

"Can I ride in the truck?"

"Only if you let me take you on a date first." Kelly was stunned that those words had tumbled so freely from her mouth, shocked that she'd even asked her the question. Asking a woman trapped beneath a ton of bricks and debris to go out with her was crazy. What the hell was she doing? Sometimes, being impulsive turned out to be embarrassing and not the smartest thing at all.

"A date? Seriously?"

"Sure. Why not?" Might as well go for it. There was something about Talia that Kelly felt drawn to.

"Um, okay."

Kelly started to reply, but the noise started up again and

drowned out her words. After a few moments, it was quiet again. She moved the blanket back to check on the progress. A sliver of light shone in above them and several gloved hands were moving debris. The hole quickly grew until it was large enough for someone to look in.

The first face she saw was Scott's.

"'Bout damn time," she said.

"Bite me," he said. "Just a couple more feet and we'll be able to slide her out onto the back board. We can see through now and her leg's pinned under a tire and axel. We're going to have to lift it to move her."

Kelly now had more room to navigate. She placed her hands on either side of Talia's head. "I've got her. Let's do it." Shifting to protect as much of Talia's torso as she could, she said, "We're almost out, Talia. Just one last bit of —"

Talia said something that Kelly couldn't understand. Her eyes rolled back in her head.

Kelly panicked. Had she stopped breathing? "Shit." She felt for a pulse in her neck. It wasn't there. "She's coding!"

Kelly's words brought a flurry of activity. What seemed like a horde of firefighters scrambled to pull away chunks of rubble. They moved like madmen, superhuman, momentarily caring nothing for their own safety.

The truck creaked and shook as it lifted away, and a thousand beams of light, prisms through both broken and unbroken glass, hit Kelly in the face, temporarily blinding her.

The minute Talia's leg was free Scott was there to help Kelly slide her onto a long, hard plastic board. Kelly felt like she was in a dream. She was moving in rhythm with the other paramedics, doing her job like she was on auto-pilot. Give meds, start CPR, defibrillate. It all ran together so fast. She couldn't keep track of everything.

Another firefighter cutting away Talia's pants suddenly yelled that Talia was bleeding. Kelly looked up from the medication she was giving to see a pool of blood oozing all over the board and immediately realized what was happening.

She pushed the man out of her way and straddled Talia's legs, placing her hands over the femoral artery just above Talia's knee. "Arterial bleed! Let's move!" She used all her strength to apply enough pressure to get the bleeding to stop.

"Ok guys," Jimmy said. He was somewhere close, but Kelly couldn't see him. "Lift the backboard and get it on that stretcher. McCoy, you keep pressure on that artery and get the hell out of here."

Kelly focused on her hands, balancing as best as she could and careful not to move off the artery as the backboard was carried to the stretcher. Scott was there to make sure she didn't fall off.

A man dressed in a nice suit with a horrified look on his face followed. As they neared the ambulance, he rushed to the stretcher and took Talia's hand. "I'm here, darlin'. I'm right here."

"We'll take care of her, Jacob," Kelly said. Her colleagues rolled the stretcher toward the waiting ambulance. The last thing Kelly saw before the bus doors slammed shut was the man falling to his knees, crying.

Chapter
Four

KELLY STRADDLED THE cot as they rolled into the emergency room. She continued to press down on the ruptured femoral artery in Talia's mangled leg, her strong hands holding back the blood. Kelly's slacks were wet and her knees felt warm and sticky. Her wrists tensed to the point of pain, but she never considered letting up the pressure. She let her fellow medics give the vitals so she could concentrate.

"Her right leg is partially severed above the knee," one of the other paramedics informed the doctor as they wheeled the cot into the trauma bay. "We've got all other bleeding under control. Blood pressure is seventy over palp. Pulse is weak and thready."

"She lost consciousness," Kelly said, "as soon as the weight was lifted off her."

"How long was she trapped?" the doctor asked.

"About an hour and a half," one of the paramedics said. "She coded during extrication, but we got her back. She was down about two minutes."

Sweat dripped from Kelly's forehead and into her eyes. "Can I get some help here with pressure?"

The doctor said, "Hang on. Just one sec..."

Kelly let her gaze rest on Talia's pale face. She ceased to pay attention to the flurry of activity around her. She didn't need to. She'd been a paramedic long enough to know what was happening and to trust that the team would do all they could to save Talia's life.

"Get me a tourniquet on that leg," the doctor said. "Clamp!"

While someone called for a surgeon, nurses worked to remove clothing with practiced efficiency. The other paramedics milled about doing whatever they could to help. One of them offered to take over for her, but Kelly vehemently told him no. She wasn't going to let go of Talia.

A nurse took Talia's vitals and announced that her blood pressure and pulse rate had dropped. Her breathing was more ragged despite the oxygen mask.

"Don't go," Kelly whispered. "Not yet. Please."

The doctor bent over Talia's leg and applied a surgical clamp on the torn artery. "You can let go now."

"I don't want to let go." Kelly was surprised to hear the shaking in her own voice.

"It's okay." Two of the other firefighters helped Kelly down from the cot.

The doctor asked, "Any idea how much blood she's lost?"

Someone Kelly couldn't see responded, "Close to 900 cc's. She's got two liters of normal saline on board."

"Call for whole blood, then let's get her to the OR, stat!"

Kelly stumbled backwards as the team of nurses and doctors worked to get Talia out of the emergency room. Scott's strong arms were suddenly holding her up. "C'mon partner," he said. "Let's get you taken care of."

"I'm okay."

"Sure you are. Except that your head is bleeding and you look like hell."

THE WAITING AREA for the emergency room was crowded with people. Many had to stand since every chair was taken. Scott wheeled Kelly through, on the way to the exit, but before they could get to the door, a little Irish woman in jeans and a brown top pushed everyone aside. Marina McCoy's hair was brick red, and her face held such anguish that Kelly nearly cried.

"I'm fine, Ma."

"You're not fine." Marina knelt beside the wheel chair and took Kelly's face into her hands. "How bad is it? Someone said you have a concussion."

"I—"

Scott spoke over her. "She has ten stitches on the side of her head and no, there's no concussion. She's got a damn hard head. The doc said to keep an eye on her tonight and she gets a free pass from work for our next shift."

Kelly scrunched up her face at Scott as soon as Marina let go of her. "Traitor."

"Best friend," he whispered to her. To Marina he said, "Want me to help you get this stubborn broad home?"

"Yes, please," Marina said. She touched Kelly's face. "You sure there's nothing else wrong?"

Kelly held her mother's hand. "I promise."

Chapter
Five

EXHAUSTION ALLOWED KELLY to sleep until the next morning. The smell of bacon brought her out of bed and into the kitchen, where she nearly tripped over her cat, Ginger. The orange tabby was stationed at the doorway, patiently waiting to be fed.

"At least one member of the family got up on time." Marina placed a bowl on the floor in front of Ginger.

Kelly watched her pet devour her breakfast. "Where does she put it?"

"Same place you do, I imagine." Marina patted Kelly's flat belly.

Kelly noticed the array of food on the table and wondered if they were having guests over for breakfast. A full plate of bacon, scrambled eggs piled high with a stack of toast beside them was enough for the whole firehouse. "Ma, you know—"

"You're probably hungry so I figured I'd make you a decent breakfast. I took off work for a few days so I can make sure you relax."

"I'm going to the hospital today."

"Why? Is something wrong?" Her mother sounded so anxious that Kelly let out a sigh.

"No, no. Ma, sit down, please." Kelly waited for Marina to settle into her chair. "I want to visit Talia. I need to make sure she's okay."

"She's stable."

"How do you know?"

"Because Scott called while you were asleep. He figured you'd want to know." Marina waved at Kelly's empty plate. "Now eat before your breakfast gets cold."

Kelly loaded up her plate, though she didn't feel so hungry. All she could think about was Talia. Would she be okay? Would she lose her leg? Would she even remember Kelly when she woke up? The stress of the injuries and trauma often wiped people's memories. It hurt to think that Talia wouldn't remember her. What would Kelly do then?

She must have been picking at her food because Marina took the fork out of her hand. "What?" Kelly asked.

"Exactly. Tell me what's going on in that head of yours."

"I was just thinking about Talia." Kelly leaned her elbows on the table and rested her chin in her hands. "I can't explain it, Ma. I just need to see for myself that she's okay."

"You went through a hellish experience with her. You don't need to explain anything." Marina smoothed back Kelly's hair. "Just promise me something."

"What?"

"Don't fall for her."

"What?" Kelly straightened in her chair. "Ma, she's just a patient."

"I know that look in your eyes, Kelly Marie. You be careful. I don't want you getting hurt again."

She was talking about Janine, and Kelly groaned. That woman was the worst mistake she'd ever made. As buddies they were okay. As lovers they were dynamite...as in explosive and dangerous. "I'll be careful."

"Good. Now finish your breakfast."

KELLY STOOD AT the corner window and let out a deep breath, her shoulders sagging. She'd been in the hospital room all day, watching over Talia who laid so still, her brown skin mottled with cuts and bruises. The monitors assured her that Talia's vital signs were stable, but didn't explain why she hadn't yet awakened.

The doctor said Talia might be slow to come out of the anesthetic after the long surgery. Or she could have slipped into a coma so her body could heal itself. The body could be amazing in that respect.

The bed and its wounded occupant were reflected into the window from which Kelly peered. She asked herself again why she was at this woman's side. A woman she didn't know.

No, that last part wasn't true. She felt a connection with Talia. Kelly couldn't explain it, but something in her gut kept her there, patiently waiting for her to wake up.

She turned from the window and stood next to the bed to take another look at the woman who had been trapped beneath the truck.

Talia carried several pounds more than necessary, a fact that may have saved her life. She was a big woman, very tall, with black hair that curled around full cheeks. Kelly brushed her fingers across Talia's forehead, pushing her bangs back. The skin felt warm. She moved her hand to Talia's. She thought for a moment that Talia gripped back, but it was only her imagination.

"I don't know what it is about you, Talia Stoddard, but I have a feeling we're going to be stuck with one other. I hope you don't mind having a new friend."

Kelly squeezed her hand a little, released it and sat in the chair beside the bed. She leaned her arms against the rail and said, "I'll be here when you wake up."

TWENTY-FOUR HOURS had never seemed so long to Kelly. Maybe because it was her first shift back from injury leave. Or maybe it was because she couldn't keep her mind off a certain woman lying in a hospital room across town.

She wanted to check on Talia. A nurse friend of Kelly's had made sure she was kept up to date on Talia's condition, but Kelly felt something tugging inside to see for herself. She wanted to touch Talia's hand and know she was okay.

Kelly got into her car and was glad there was very little traffic. Rush hour was over and she made it to the hospital in record time._ Parking was even easier and when the elevator opened when she hit the button, Kelly smiled. The luck of the Irish, her father would say.

A few steps down two corridors, one more ride up another floor and she was there. Kelly paused in front of the door of Talia's hospital room to adjust the collar on her teal golf shirt. She brushed off some invisible lint, glanced at the small bouquet of wildflowers held in the crook of her left arm, and pushed the door open.

Quiet steps brought her to Talia's bedside. She placed the flowers in the empty vase on the nightstand and turned her attention to the woman on the bed. Tubes and wires attached to strategic points on her body, all of them monitoring her vital functions and reassuring Kelly that Talia was still alive. She glanced up at the monitor to her right.

"Sinus rhythm," she muttered. "Good to see your heart is working well." Kelly looked over the rest of the numbers on the monitor, satisfied Talia was stable. "Still not awake I see."

Kelly pulled a chair close to the bed and sat, her left hand covering Talia's. "I was hoping you'd be up and about today. It's been almost a week, ya know?"

She brushed a few strands of dark hair off Talia's face. "But I guess your body needs the time to heal." Kelly brought the hand to her lips and placed a soft kiss across the knuckles. "I know you can hear me, so I'm going to tell you to hurry up and get better. I'd love the chance to see those gorgeous eyes again."

The creak of the door startled Kelly, and she whirled around in her seat. An older woman walked in. She was tall, her skin the color of chocolate, and her piercing gaze made Kelly nervous.

"Are you a friend of Talia's?"

"Oh, I — uh..." Kelly stood, releasing her hold on Talia's hand. "Sort of."

"Sort of?" The woman approached the bed. "Either you are or you aren't. Which is it?"

Kelly melted under the woman's intense gaze. She sat in the chair Kelly had just vacated as though she were the queen of the hospital and the seat was her throne. "I'm a friend, though we haven't known each other long."

"Do you work with her?"

"No, ma'am. I was—I'm part of the team of firefighters who pulled her out from under the truck and all the rubble ." The woman remained eerily silent, and Kelly sensed that was bad. "I've been checking on her progress—to see how she's—"

"You were there?" The woman's eyes were so intense Kelly couldn't look away. "You were there when my daughter was almost killed?"

Her words felt like an accusation, and Kelly didn't know how to react. "Well, no. I arrived afterwards. I was one of the first ones there—"

"Why didn't you get her out in time?" Her gaze never wavered, pinning Kelly in place.

"We did get her out in time."

"Not good enough." She reached out and put Talia's hand into her own. "She's my only daughter and, because of you, I may lose her."

"No, please, that's not true. The doctors say she'll come out of this."

"No thanks to you." Mrs. Stoddard turned away from Kelly to gaze at her daughter.

Kelly's throat went dry. "Mrs. Stoddard? I have your name right, don't I?"

Her only response was a single nod.

"There wasn't anything more that could have been done. Our team extricated Talia as quickly as possible. You have to understand—"

"I don't have to understand anything. Now please leave."

"I—"

"Now." Mrs. Stoddard's stern voice left Kelly no options. She turned on her heel and left the room. Once in the hallway, she leaned against the wall and let out a deep breath.

Chapter
Six

KELLY EASED THROUGH the front door of the house, hoping not to wake her mother. Marina was a light sleeper and got cranky when she worked third shift at McAfferty's Grocery and got home at eight a.m. Kelly only got two steps into the foyer before she heard her mother's voice.

"Where have you been? It's nearly three o'clock in the afternoon. I know you got off shift at seven because I called the station." Marina stood at the end of the foyer, her pink cotton robe wrapped tightly around her. "Why didn't you call?"

"I didn't think about it. I had a lot on my mind." She dropped her keys on the entryway table and walked the few steps to her mother. "I'm sorry."

Marina narrowed her eyes. "You know how I worry, Kelly Marie."

"Ma, please." Kelly gave her a quick hug and slipped past to head for the kitchen. "I really don't want to have a fight with you right now."

"Who's fighting?" Marina spun around to follow Kelly, shooing her from the refrigerator. "Sit down. I'll fix you something decent to eat."

"Thanks," Kelly said. She lowered herself to a chair at the yellow table. Her fingers idly traced one of the many orange and red flowers that decorated the Formica top. She didn't hear her mother's comment. "I'm sorry. What did you say?"

"I asked if you went to the hospital today." Marina placed a steaming plate of food in front of Kelly. "Did you talk to Talia?"

"No. Well, sort of." Kelly said. Her mother waited patiently for more information. "Her mother showed up."

"Isn't that a good thing?"

Kelly shrugged, pushing around the food on her plate with her fork. "I was sitting with Talia. She's not awake yet, and I was talking to her. I brought her flowers."

"That's sweet, darling, but it doesn't tell me much." Marina leaned forward and placed her hand over the hand Kelly was using to play with her food. "What did Talia's mother say to you?"

"She doesn't think we got Talia freed soon enough. She blames us—me—for her daughter being unconscious."

"And how were you supposed to get her out any faster?" Marina asked. "It took almost two hours."

"Yeah. I would have told her that, but she'd just have gotten more pissed. She didn't give me a chance to explain that if we'd gone any faster, the whole thing could have come down on her and me."

"Not an option."

"I know." Kelly looked up at Marina. "She made me feel like it was my fault. I've run that rescue in my head over and over, Ma. I can't think of anything we could have done differently."

"You sound so much like your father." Marina patted her daughter's shoulder. "He always did that, but he rarely found anything that he could have done differently, not anything that would have changed the outcome. You all got her out alive. You did what you were supposed to do. You can't control if she survives, and God willing she will. Ignore her mother. She's wrong."

"That's so easy to say."

"Even easier to do. Stop thinking about what you could have done, Kelly Marie. You did your job, and that's that. Now tell me the real reason you keep going to see Talia."

"I go see her because I'm curious about her recovery. I remind myself that she's going to make it. You know we hardly ever get to find out how our patients do in the long run."

"Uh huh," Marina said. "I'd buy that if I didn't know you. You've got enough contacts at the hospital that you could call any time and find out how she's doing. I want the truth. Are you interested in her?"

"Ma!"

"Don't 'Ma' me. You're interested. Is she pretty?"

"What? No. I mean, she's not especially pretty, I guess. Overweight. And how the hell could I be interested in her?" Kelly was protesting despite the fact that she felt the telltale blush on her cheeks. "I don't know anything about this woman. She's a patient of mine."

"A patient you spent nearly two extremely stressful hours with. You can't expect me to believe you didn't talk to her." Marina got up to get some coffee. "You're my daughter, after all. You may be a lot like your father, Kelly Marie, but when it comes to talking, you're my kid all the way."

"Oh, geez." Kelly buried her face in her hands. "I got to like her, sure. But that's it. I seriously want to see how she does. That's it."

"Sure. No problem." Marina took her full cup of coffee and headed out of the kitchen. On the way, she patted Kelly's head. "I've got night shift again tonight. Be a good girl and finish your food. It's your turn to do the dishes."

Chapter
Seven

TALIA HEARD VOICES, but her eyes refused to open and her mouth would not speak. She could make her fingers twitch, but her whole body seemed to ignore any brain command to move. Fuzzy-headed and exhausted, she couldn't tell if she was dreaming or not.

"When will my daughter awaken?"

That voice pierced the haze. Why was her mother here?

A man replied in a calm voice, "We aren't sure, Mrs. Stoddard. At this point it's up to Talia. When her body has healed enough—"

"What about her leg?" Colette Stoddard launched into a high-pitched voice that was more like a screech. The sound hurt Talia's ears. "How long will the recovery be?"

"It's hard to say right now. We have to make sure Talia heals from the surgery. Your daughter has been through a lot. We had to remove her spleen and repair her left kidney."

"No thanks to that maniac in the truck. I'm glad he's dead."

"Mrs. Stoddard, we should—"

"What kind of life would she have with one leg?"

"Your daughter is a healthy young woman. If we have to take her leg, she'll recover. We'll give her physical therapy. She'll get a prosthetic leg and in a few months should be walking like normal."

"No. Normal is no longer part of her life."

Talia heard the distinct sound of high heels clicking on the tile floor. She wanted to say something to the man with the kind voice. What about her leg? Why couldn't she wake up? What was going on?

A rapid beeping hurt her ears, and Talia heard movement around her. The doctor spoke, but she couldn't make out his words. It was hard to breathe and her chest felt ready to explode.

Her eyes fluttered open as someone leaned over her, the woman's calm voice whispering, "It's all right, hon. We've got you."

Talia closed her eyes and fell into a deep sleep.

WHEN SHE AWOKE again, Talia was first aware of the soreness in her throat. She moved her lips and tried to swallow, but her mouth felt like sandpaper. She tried to talk and only managed to produce a squeak.

"Hi there," a woman said. Talia couldn't see her. "Would you like some ice chips?"

Talia nodded and the woman, who she assumed was a nurse, spooned a few of the chips into her mouth. The ice melted, soothing her throat. "Thanks," she croaked.

"You're welcome. I'm Jody, and I'm your nurse today."

"Has anyone been here?"

"Yes. Your mother. Every day since she arrived last week."

"My — mother?"

"Mmm hmm." Jody slipped a blood pressure cuff on Talia's arm. "She ought to be here anytime. Later tonight Kelly should be by. Probably around ten or so."

"Kelly?"

Jody made a few notations on a clipboard, and checked the IV that flowed into Talia's left arm. "Yeah, but don't tell anyone we let her up here. Apparently your Mother doesn't want her around."

"Wait. Was she here recently? Talking to a doctor? My mother, I mean." Talia tried to force the memory to the surface. "Something about my leg. They were talking about me, but all I remember is Mother arguing with him."

"Ah, that was yesterday."

"I kinda remember it." Talia wiped the sleep from her eyes. "Can I sit up?"

"Sure, let me raise the bed."

Talia waited until the bed was at a tilt and asked Jody to stop. "Guess I'm too sore to sit up much."

"That's to be expected. I've got some meds to give you. One of them is for pain. It'll make you sleepy."

Talia winced when she tried to adjust to a new position. "I think I'd prefer the sleep."

"Thought so."

"Thanks." Talia chewed the ice and let it melt and soothe her throat. "Can you do me a favor?"

"Sure."

"Can you make it so visitors are allowed in here, regardless of what my mother says?"

"You're the patient. What you say goes."

"Do you know if anyone called my dad or my brothers?"

"I don't know. I did see a man at the end of my shift last night, but I didn't talk to him. I'll check with the other nurses."

"Thanks."

"You have a phone. I can turn on the ringer if you want."

"That would be fantastic," Talia said. "I can call them when I wake up."

THE LIGHT WAS intense and Talia regretted opening her eyes.

She gave her fuzzy mind a few moments to register what had happened. Hospital. The unmistakable smell of antiseptic and a pine-scented cleaner reminded her where she was. She could remember the nurse visiting, but how long ago was that?

Her mind drew a blank. "Damn," she muttered.

"Well, not the hello I was expecting."

Talia turned, aware of every second of pounding pain that came with the movement. The pair of green eyes that stared back startled her. There was something so very familiar about them. The woman's smile touched her heart. "Who?"

"Kelly McCoy. I'm the paramedic that was with you."

"Oh, I remember you now."

"Yep. Just came to see how you're doing."

"My leg doesn't hurt as much as it did."

A man in a white lab coat joined them. "Hi, Talia. I'm Doctor Anthony James. I've got you on morphine right now, but I can change that if you need me to." He opened Talia's chart.

"So what's my prognosis?" Talia asked.

He looked up from the clipboard and studied her a moment. "We removed your spleen and were able to repair your left kidney. The artery in your left thigh was compromised when your lower leg was crushed."

"But I'll be okay?"

"You'll be hospitalized for a while longer, but overall you're fine. However, I'm going to be honest and tell you that the odds of saving your leg are not good."

Talia felt like someone had knocked the wind out of her. She looked at Kelly, but she remained focused on the doctor.

"Why?" Talia asked. "What's wrong with it?"

"The leg sustained a great deal of damage and was without blood flow for far too long. Infection set in, and we can't allow it to spread."

"Can't you just give me antibiotics? There must be some medicine."

The doctor launched into a long description full of medical terminology that went completely over her head. He finished by saying, "But we're monitoring it, and we won't act precipitously."

"So what are you saying—there's a chance it'll heal?" Talia asked. She was afraid not to be optimistic, but at the same time, a terrible feeling had come over her.

"There's always a chance. No matter what happens, you're going to need surgery on the leg as soon as you're well enough."

"How long will that be?" Talia asked.

"A couple of days. I'm going to have an orthopedic surgeon stop by later today. Her name is Dr. Lin and she's the best we have." Dr.

James hung the chart at the foot of her bed. "Talia, I don't want to discourage you. Even if you do lose the leg, we've got the technology today to have you up and walking again in a few months. A year from now no one would be able to tell if you have a prosthetic leg."

"You sound like you're sure that amputation is the next step, no pun intended."

"I'm just making sure you know the options." He smiled and stepped away from the bedside to leave. "You never know. You might end up with a bionic leg."

Kelly waited until he was gone to speak. "That could be cool."

"What? A bionic leg?"

"Sure. You could really kick some ass then."

Talia yawned and felt her eyes getting heavy. "Right now I feel too tired to kick anything."

"It's the meds. Close your eyes and rest. I'll be by tomorrow afternoon."

"Promise?"

"Of course."

KELLY ARRIVED THE next afternoon, but hesitated going into Talia's room. She was sure she heard Mrs. Stoddard's voice.

"From the look on your face, I assume you've already met the Queen Mother. I was hoping I'd catch you before you had the horror of that experience. " A man wearing an expensive, dark gray suit approached. She thought she recognized him, but couldn't think of his name.

"If you're referring to Mrs. Stoddard —"

"Let me introduce myself," he said, holding out his hand. "Jacob Meier."

"Of course. I thought you looked familiar. You're Talia's friend."

"She's my best friend in the world. And I'm glad she had some 'family' to take care of her. Makes me feel better. She's so special. I wish I could find a nice woman like you for her."

Kelly was surprised at his candor. But not surprised that he was gay. "Well, that's handy to know I suppose."

"Of course it is." Jacob took her by the arm and led her down the hallway toward the elevators. "Let's get out of here before the Queen Mother comes out of the room. She's been staying until around five, so we can come back later."

"Sure," Kelly said. "I guess I'll just have to make myself busy until after five."

They got into the elevator and Jacob pressed the Lobby button. "Well, I've got to get back to the office. What do you say we meet later for dinner and we'll go see Talia together?"

"Sounds like a plan."

They exchanged cell phone numbers. Jacob said, "I think it's very sweet that you've been visiting her so much."

"How'd you know I've been here and how'd you know I'd be here this afternoon?"

Jacob's glance led her to the information desk as they walked past it to the front doors. A handsome, young man was seated behind the desk and waved to them. "I have my ways."

DINNER AND AN hour of conversation went by quickly. Kelly found Jacob charming and entertaining. She laughed so much her sides hurt. Now back at the hospital, she corralled her merry mood. The elevator door opened and they headed for Talia's room.

"You're killing me," she said. "Tell me again why you're single? You're a delightful guy to be around."

"I'm single on purpose. Relationships make me itch."

"I sort of expected you to say that." Kelly took a long breath and let it out slowly. "Damn. You and all your jokes. You made my abs hurt."

"That's because you've never had the pleasure of my humor. Trust me, you'll get used to it and do the same thing Talia does."

"Which is?"

Jacob did his best impression of a high, feminine voice: "Jacob, stop it. I can't laugh any more."

A voice called out, "I don't say that."

Jacob and Kelly entered Talia's room. She was sitting up and had finished a bowl of what looked like soup. Or at least something liquid and yellowish.

"Yes, you do," Jacob said and sat on the edge of the bed. "You said that just yesterday when I was here."

"Because I have stitches, and it hurts to laugh." Talia turned to Kelly. "Help?"

Kelly held her hands up in a gesture of surrender. "Nope. I'm Switzerland. You two get to work this one out. I'm just here for the company."

"Gee, thanks." Talia stuck her lower lip out. "Nice to have friends."

Kelly placed her finger on the outturned lip and said, "This look has to go. Doesn't really work for you."

Talia's mouth formed a thin line.

"Nope. That one's no good either."

Talia frowned.

"Still not right." Kelly used her index fingers to form the edges of Talia's mouth into a smile. "Ah, now that's the look I was after."

"Ha ha." Talia stuck her tongue out and dodged when Kelly made a grab for it. "Be nice."

"I am nice. Just ask Jacob."

Talia narrowed her gaze at Jacob. "Oh?"

"Nice enough to let me buy her dinner," he said and looked at his watch. "Oh, look at the time. Gotta run. I'll leave you in Miss Thing's capable hands." He gave Kelly a meaningful look and kissed Talia on the cheek before backing out of the room doing a graceful little dance to the door.

Talia shook her head. "He does that when he doesn't want to tell me something."

"It wasn't a big deal," Kelly said. "We just met at the cafeteria for a bite to eat before coming up here."

"And he told you all about me, right?"

"Pretty much."

"I'll kill him."

"Um, could you wait to kill him? I'd like to take you on that date I promised, and if you're in jail for murder, it would be kinda tough."

"Oh, sure. I'll wait." Talia looked down at her hands and Kelly sensed something was wrong. "You don't have to, you know."

"Have to what?"

"Take me out on the obligatory date."

"Well, I've never dated anyone in jail, but I guess I could give it a go." Kelly made light of it, but if Talia was trying to steer her away from the promised date, that wasn't going to happen. Kelly really wanted to know this woman better and she wasn't about to renege on her promise. She took hold of Talia's hand. "If it's all the same to you, I'd like to plan the date for us."

"What do you have in mind?" Talia still wouldn't look up at her.

"Well, dinner and maybe a movie. If there's nothing at the cinema, we can always rent a DVD or watch *Star Wars* again. It'd be about number 320 for me. How 'bout you?"

"At least that many," Talia said.

Kelly leaned down so she could see Talia's face. "I'm serious. I think it'd be fun. And if it's going to take too long for you to get out of here, I'll just bring the DVD to you."

Talia's eyes met Kelly's and Kelly was sure there was an extra sparkle to them. "Promise to bring food, and I'll let you have the date tomorrow."

"That's my girl." Kelly kissed her hand before releasing it. "Actually, I have to work tomorrow, but I'll set it up for the first afternoon I have off. An impromptu date. Though I still plan to keep you to the real one when you get out. Okay?"

"Sounds prefect."

"Excellent." Kelly said. "I need to head home so my mother doesn't think I've run off to join the circus."

Chapter
Eight

THE HOSPITAL ROOM was silent when Kelly walked in. The lights were off and she figured Talia was asleep. She put the flowers down on the bedside table.

"You don't have to be quiet," Talia said. "I've been awake for a while."

"Well, you should be asleep. It's not even eight yet." Kelly said. "The sun is barely awake."

"The sun isn't doped up with morphine and getting woke up every couple of hours by a nurse."

"There is that." Kelly leaned on the bed rail. "So, grumpy much?"

Talia laughed. "Every morning."

"I got you flowers."

"Oh, how sweet!" Talia carefully turned so she could see them. "White roses. No one's ever given me roses before."

"They're for friendship."

Before she could elaborate, movement at the door caught her eye, and a man entered. He wore a Marine dress uniform. He was tall, muscular and had skin darker than Talia's.

He said, "I'm out of the country for a couple of months and look what happens."

Talia let out a shriek and held open her arms. He launched across the room and gathered her carefully to him.

"Sam! When did you get in?"

He pulled back from his hug and kissed her on the forehead. "About an hour ago. Caught a taxi here soon as I landed."

"I thought you were in Germany. Don't tell me you've been deployed again?"

"When Mother called, I got leave and hopped the first plane to the states." He smiled and nodded toward Kelly. "Care to make introductions?"

"Oh, I'm sorry." Talia patted Kelly's hand. "Kelly, this is my big brother, Sam. He's a captain with the Marines. Kelly is the firefighter who saved my life."

"Well, one of the firefighters," Kelly said, taking Sam's offered hand.

"Great to meet you. Thanks for taking care of Little T."

Talia hit his arm. "Don't call me that."

"Why not?" He chuckled. "It's been your name since you were born."

"I hate you."

"No, you don't."

"So this is what it's like to have a brother?" Kelly asked. "I don't feel so left out anymore."

"Trust me," Talia said. "You're not missing anything."

Sam started to respond, but Talia held up her hand to quiet him. The look on his face was comical and they all laughed.

"I'll let you two visit," Kelly said.

"Call me later?" Talia asked.

"Of course." Kelly waved to them on her way out.

"Hmm, nice," Sam said.

"What?" Talia asked.

"Nice everything. I think you've got a winner there, T."

"Sam Stoddard, what makes you so certain I have anything with her?"

"Want the whole list or just the top ten?"

She hit his arm. "She's just a friend. Besides, women like her don't go for women like me."

"Ah, so you've already figured out she's gay?" He ducked her next punch. "You work quickly."

"Why are you here again?"

"To make sure my baby sister is okay." He took hold of her hand. "Are you? Doing okay, that is?"

"The doctor says I'm all right."

"Mother told me your leg was crushed. I'd like to see it, if you don't mind." She hesitated, and he said, "I've seen the worst of battle wounds, T. Just show me."

She said, "It's wrapped, but you can see how awful my foot looks."

He helped her pull back the covers. "Yeah, it doesn't look good, does it."

"No." Talia motioned his hands away. "It hurts all the time."

"What did the doc say about it?"

"Not much. That they still may have to amputate it. They don't want to do anything that's not life threatening until my body has had time to heal."

"Mother didn't tell me that."

"She probably didn't tell you she called Megan."

"Why the hell did she do that? You don't need that bitch." Sam looked like he wanted to say more, but Talia understood he was holding back. "I'm sorry. I just don't get why she'd call her. You two broke up over a year ago."

"Mother thinks she's my best bet for a safe and happy life, if I insist on being gay, that is. And since Megan calls Mother more than she ever called me, I shouldn't be surprised. I expect she'll be here any day now."

"Want me to set up security for you?"

Talia laughed, not sure if he was serious or not. Sam was protective enough to post a troop of marines at her door. "Not necessary. I'll figure out how to handle Megan."

"Just make sure you don't fall back into that same crap with her, okay?"

For ten years Talia had been back and forth with Megan in their tumultuous relationship. She felt she had to have Megan to feel okay about herself. As long as she was with someone, Talia felt normal. Alone, she felt unprotected and scared. Sam was the one who pulled her away from Megan and helped her reconnect with her college friend, Jacob.

"I'll do my best," Talia said. "Besides, I've got Jacob to kick my butt if need be."

"Knock, knock." a cheery voice sang out.

Sam smiled. "Impeccable timing as always."

"You expect anything else?" Talia asked. She was happy to see him bounce into the room. Her two favorite men in one place.

"Oh! Hiya soldier boy." Jacob said, heading right for Sam with his arms opened wide. "Hmmm, I do love a man in uniform."

Sam stood and offered his hand to Jacob, politely avoiding a hug. "Nice to see you again."

"You have no idea." His eyes looked Sam up and down.

"Jacob! Stop that." Talia grabbed a brightly wrapped box out of his hands. "There better be chocolate in this box."

"Honey, I'm your best friend. Would I bring you anything else?"

They shared a laugh as she opened the gift. "Almond?" Talia asked.

"You know it."

Talia popped one in her mouth and savored the candy, licking her fingertips clean. "Mmm. If you were a woman, I'd marry you."

"That's because I'm irresistible."

"And, you bring chocolate."

"That, too." Jacob settled in a chair next to Sam. "So, has your dad been by yet today? I saw him in the waiting room yesterday and he said he had a meeting to attend, and I promised to call him if anything changed. We figured your mother wasn't going to call him."

"I haven't seen Daddy yet. Mother's been in and out a lot, though." Talia chewed on another piece of chocolate. "Mmm. What about Aaron?"

"Aaron will fly in on Friday." Colette Stoddard made her usual grand entrance and took the box of candy from Talia. "Keep eating that candy, and you'll not only get acne, but you'll gain more weight. You should know better than to give her those, Jacob."

"It's a pleasure to see you, too, Colette."

"Hello, Mother." Sam stood and gave her a hug.

"You were supposed to call me to pick you up when you arrived, Sam." Colette hugged him.

"Sorry. I spotted a cab when I got to baggage claim and decided to come here directly. Save you the trouble of getting me."

"You're never any trouble, son." Colette patted his cheek and sat where Sam had been.

Jacob rose and kissed Talia on the cheek. "I'll see you tomorrow."

"Thanks," Talia said, looking longingly at the box of chocolates now out of reach.

Jacob winked at Sam and hurried out of the room.

Talia waited for the door to close before addressing her mother. "You should be nicer to him, Mother. He's my best friend."

"You need more friends."

"No, I don't."

"You shouldn't eat sweets so soon after having major surgery."

"I'm sure you're right." Better to agree than argue, Talia figured.

Chapter
Nine

THE FLOOR OF the fire house bay hadn't been cleaner in years. Kelly was restless and had spent the last two hours scrubbing the floor. There hadn't been a single run and she was only eight hours into her shift. It was unusual to be so quiet and she was getting anxious.

The intercom buzzed and the sound echoed in the bay, startling her. A male voice announced, "McCoy, call on line two."

Feeling the need for space and privacy, Kelly hurried out of the kitchen to use the phone in the bay. "McCoy."

"Hi, Kelly."

She froze when she heard Talia's voice. "Hi."

"Sorry to call you at work. Is this a bad time?"

"Um. No. I'm just a little surprised is all. How'd you get this number?"

"I looked it up. Had to call a couple of stations before I found someone who knew you."

"Only a couple? There are a few thousand firefighters in the department," Kelly said. "So, what's up?"

"I was wondering if you could stop by today."

"I'm on a twenty-four hour shift. I don't get off work until seven tomorrow morning. I could come over then."

A pregnant pause filled the air between them. "Uh, sure. That'd be great."

"Is there something wrong?"

"Not really."

Kelly picked up on the quiet voice. "Talia, you can talk to me if you need to. Even if it has to be by phone."

"Thanks, but it's not that."

"Then what is it?"

Another pause, this one longer than before. "I want some company. I can't stand to be alone."

Kelly had no idea what to say to that. There's nothing she wanted more at that moment than to be with Talia. She'd been in Kelly's thoughts all day. "I'm sorry I can't get there right now. But starting tomorrow morning, I'm off for two days and have no plans. Will that work for you?"

"Don't do this just to appease me."

"Are you kidding? If you think I'd turn down the chance to hang out with a gorgeous woman, even if she's in the hospital, you're nuts."

Talia laughed softly. "You're the one who's nuts. But I accept your offer."

"Good. It's the best one I've got."

"And it's the best one I've had all day." Talia's voice sounded lighter, happier. "See you tomorrow?"

"You bet." Kelly waited for her to hang up before placing the receiver on the hook.

"Got a date?"

Kelly punched Scott in the arm as he walked past. "No."

He grabbed his arm and feigned pain. "Hey, you big brute."

"Whatever."

"You going to see her tomorrow?"

"What's it to you?"

"A lot."

Kelly stopped and looked back to find the rest of the guys "casually" watching through the kitchen doorway. "How much?"

"What?" Scott sounded innocent, but Kelly knew better.

"How much was the bet?"

"Bet? Oh, Kelly, you know we don't gamble on city property. That would be against the law."

"Uh-huh." She winked at the gathered men before turning back to Scott. "No date."

"Are you sure? You're going to see her, right?"

"It's a visit, Scott. Not a date. Sorry pal, you lose."

Laughter erupted behind them and Kelly strutted away, despite Scott's yelling, "Hey! It is so a date. You're going to see her, you'll be alone. It's a date."

Kelly opened her mouth to reply, and the station tones sounded. They all quieted to listen. A car accident at the intersection of Race and Fourth Streets.

"It's not a date." Kelly ran to her rack to get her gear, then hustled for the truck.

Scott was right behind her, and they both climbed into the rescue truck together. "It's a date."

"Scott, a date consists of doing something together — like going out to eat or to a movie. Not sitting in a hospital room watching the other person sleep."

"You watch her sleep?" he asked as they pulled out of the station.

"She's gone through a lot, so yeah, sometimes I watch her sleep." Kelly zipped up her coat and put her helmet on.

"But why?"

Kelly shrugged and looked away, far too aware of the blush

creeping up her cheeks. "Because I like to be with her. Besides, she feels better if someone's there when she wakes up."

"Aw, isn't that sweet?" Scott nudged her and Kelly hit him again. "You're violent."

"You haven't seen violence yet."

He started to comment, but her look shut him up.

THE SUN WAS setting on what must have been a lovely day. Talia stared out her hospital window and wished she was able to enjoy the weather. She preferred autumn to summer, but this year the temperatures hadn't been too bad. Cincinnati was usually hot, hazy, and humid. Lately it had been cool and dry.

The last time Talia remembered enjoying the weather was before the accident. She and Jacob had gone out for lunch, and he convinced her to walk to Fountain Square. He'd said it would be good for her. By the time they'd made the five-block trek, Talia was out of breath.

"I hate you, Jacob Meier."

"You always say that," Jacob said and pulled out a chair for her, one of those plastic, outdoor chairs that didn't look very sturdy. Talia was worried she'd break it, but too tired to really care. She gently settled herself into the seat, feeling the armrests dig into her thighs. "I don't think I even want to eat now."

"You need to. Not eating is worse than over-eating."

"When did you start working for Weight Watchers?"

Jacob handed her a menu. "I'm your best friend. It's my job to help you out. You need to get healthier, and I've decided to be your new coach."

"My coach?"

"Yes. Someone needs to kick your ass into gear." He took her hand and kissed the back of it. "I love you, sweetie. All of you. But it's your health I'm worried about. I don't care if you lose weight, but I do care that walking a few blocks nearly puts you into cardiac arrest."

"It's not like I enjoy this." She sat back, feeling defeated. "I just can't ever stick to a diet."

"Ugh. Diet is 'die' with a 't' on the end. No dieting. Just cut back on the sweets a little and promise you'll walk with me every day at lunch."

"Every day?"

Jacob narrowed his gaze and the look on his face made Talia laugh. He said, "Every day. Sunday included. You need to get out more."

"Okay. But if I pass out, please don't call Mother."

"As if I'd ever call the Queen Mother for anything."

Talia patted his hand. "Good man."

At the time, Talia had fully intended to keep her promise to Jacob, but the accident happened, and now she wondered if she'd ever be able to walk again. She turned her gaze from the window and heard a soft voice call from the doorway, "Hello there? Anyone home?" Kelly waved, holding one hand behind her back.

"I guess I'm anyone, so yes. I'm here." Talia said. "What do you have there?"

Kelly produced a handful of yellow carnations. "Okay, so they're not roses, but I heard these are your favorites. I wanted to make up for not getting here this morning."

"That's okay. I figured you were busy."

"Heh. That's a good word for it." Kelly set the flowers in the empty vase and settled in the chair by the bed. "We were out at a fire all night long, and soon as we got back, we got called out for a train derailment. Damn car had a nasty chemical in it. Took a couple of hours for Hazmat guys to clean it up. I had to go home and crash for a while."

"You look tired. You could have called and come over another time." Talia said the words, but didn't really mean them. Kelly was there, tired or not, and Talia was happy to see her.

"Oh, no. I said I'd come, so here I am. Just wish I'd thought to call you earlier to let you know I was going to be awhile."

"No problem. Thanks for the flowers, though. You didn't have to do that."

"Of course I did. My mother taught me to bring gifts with every apology."

"How'd you know carnations are my favorite?"

"A little birdie told me."

"Jacob." Talia wondered what else he'd said.

"Yep. He spilled the beans to me the other day. He told me a lot about you."

"It figures." Talia made a mental note to speak to her dear friend about his big mouth. "Nothing bad I hope."

"I don't think so." She looked at the monitor above Talia's head. "He did tell me some, uh, personal information."

"Oh, my." Talia covered her face with her hands. "Let me guess. He made sure you know I'm gay, single, and lonely." She peaked between her fingers to find Kelly grinning. "Did he mention I was gay?"

"Several times." Kelly laughed, the sound rich, warm and contagious.

"I'll kill him later. I hope he didn't embarrass you."

"Nope. But he wasted his time." Kelly leaned on the rail of the bed. "We've already got a date planned when you get out of here."

"Oh, that. You really don't have to go out with me."

"Maybe I want to." Kelly kissed her cheek, leaving the tender skin there feeling warm and tingly.

"Okay," Talia said.

"So, now that's settled, let's talk about something else."

"Such as?"

"You already know what I do for a living. How 'bout telling me what you do."

Talia waved her off. "My job is so boring compared to yours. I'm an insurance claims manager."

"I doubt that's boring. Bet you have to deal with a lot of pissed off people."

"You don't know the half of it." Talia glanced down at her hands, folded in her lap. "I've had to tell old men they can't have surgery because they're not covered, but if they don't have the surgery they'll die. It can be a crappy job sometimes."

"That must have been hard to deal with."

"That's why I came here to work for the Winchester Group. I did my internship there just after college. They specialize in insurance for seniors."

"Where did you work before?"

"A major company that, according to the terms of my departure contract, I'm not even allowed to say the name of anymore. They were located in DC and were just a group of assholes. I wish I'd never started there."

"Mind if I ask why you did?"

"I grew up in DC, and Mother wanted me to work close to home. It was bad enough I'd gone to college here in Cincinnati. So, she knew a friend of a friend who got me the job. I hated every minute and jumped at the first chance to leave."

"You're mother seems kinda, well—"

"Pushy?"

"I didn't want to say it, but yes. Very pushy."

"That's Colette Stoddard. She's the Queen Mother as Jacob calls her."

"He mentioned that."

"Jacob and Mother have a—let's see, what shall I call it? Maybe it's best described as a Hate-Hate relationship." She grinned. "If you're lucky, you'll work your way into the same lovely arrangement. Okay, now it's your turn. Spill."

"Not much more to tell. Born and raised in Queens, New York. My dad was a fourth generation firefighter. He didn't care that I was a girl, so long as I got into the job, too."

"Queens? You don't have an accent."

"Because I worked to get rid of it." Kelly wouldn't meet her gaze. "Too many questions about 9-11. I was on the job when it happened."

"I'm sorry to hear that," Talia said. "I was in DC, but nowhere near the Pentagon. I can't even imagine what it must have been like. My mother knew a few people who were killed that day, but I'd never met them."

"I'm not good at talking about it."

"You don't have to." Talia touched the side of Kelly's face. "Unless you want to."

"Thanks." Kelly looked up and held Talia's gaze for a moment.

Talia felt the butterflies in her stomach and the familiar twinge in her chest. She was more than just attracted to this woman and she decided to change the subject before she revealed how much she wanted to kiss her. "You don't seem old enough to have been a firefighter this long."

Kelly ran a hand through her unruly short hair. "Nice compliment, but I'm thirty-four."

"And not a strand of gray in that red hair. Do you color it?"

"Does any butch color her hair?"

"Suppose not. I probably will when I get gray hair."

"Why?" Kelly rose and moved close to the bedrail to brush the hair from Talia's shoulder. "You have beautiful hair."

"Thanks. But I'm thirty-six and well on my way to a bottle of hair dye."

"Don't. God gave you a gift. So what if it changes color a little? Who cares?"

She was not real, Talia thought. How could a woman like her possibly be so—so interested in her? She was flirting. Wasn't she?

Kelly leaned down slowly, and Talia was sure she was going to kiss her. Would it be sweet? Her lips looked so soft and inviting...

"Get a room!" Jacob said.

Kelly bounced away from the bed like a pinball, and Talia smirked at her embarrassment. "You've got lousy timing, Jacob."

"That's what all the guys say." He sighed dramatically and made himself comfortable in the chair beside her bed. "So, are you two making plans for a date yet?"

"No," they chorused and laughed again. Talia shook her finger at Jacob. "Back off, Mr. Matchmaker. You hear me?"

"I hear, but I'm not listening."

Kelly's face got redder. "I need to get going. Ma's expecting me for dinner." Kelly returned to bedside and squeezed Talia's hand. "I'll give you a call later. Okay?"

"Look forward to it." Talia caught Kelly's gaze. There was something in the look she was giving her, but Kelly turned away before Talia could figure it out. Kelly waved as she hurried out of the room.

"She's one cute little butch," Jacob said.

"Shut up."

"And you're loving the attention, aren't you?"

"Shut up, Jacob."

"I mean, she's been here almost every day—even before you woke up—always at your side. She's got it bad for you. All you need to do is snap your fingers and she's yours." He snapped his fingers in the air and waggled his eyebrows at Talia. "You make a cute couple."

Talia glared, trying to be as intimidating as possible.

"You're going to be sorry if you let this one get away."

Talia opened up her mouth to speak, but he held up his hand. "I know, 'Shut up, Jacob.'"

"Good. Finally a man who can be trained."

Jacob stuck his tongue out at her and turned on the TV, ignoring her smug look.

Chapter
Ten

MEGAN BRUGGE WAS a tall, slender woman with dark hair cut into short curls that left her long face exposed. She had a round chin and soft cheeks, but there was nothing else soft about her. Talia stared at the doorway as her mother greeted Megan in the hallway, then watched her ex walk in to the hospital room. No. Walked wasn't the right word. Sauntered. Megan always moved with a purpose, like a tiger on the prowl. Talia knew enough to worry about what Megan wanted.

Talia hadn't spoken to her ex in more than a year. Thirteen months and two weeks, give or take. They'd split up after Talia had, in Jacob's words, "Grown a pair." Megan was a control freak. Always. And her need for control had finally pushed Talia to pack up and leave. It was the hardest thing she'd ever done.

Megan greeted Colette warmly, then looked toward Talia, smiled, said something else to Colette, and approached the bed. Colette left without another word, and Talia took a deep breath. Here goes.

"How are you feeling?" Megan said. Her voice was kind, but her eyes were as cold as Talia remembered.

"Sore, but doing well. The doctor says with some physical therapy I should be fine. Probably be able to go home in a few weeks."

"Good. Your mother and I were speaking about that. You going home, I mean." Megan reached for Talia's hand, but Talia tucked both her hands under the covers. "We're going to arrange a special flight for you."

"Flight? I live less than two miles from here. I won't be flying anywhere."

"Don't be naïve, Talia," Megan's tone turned to the condescending one Talia was so familiar with. "You can't possibly stay here."

"Why not? I live here"

"Yes. I'm well aware of your current location, but your sabbatical is over. It's time you came home where your family can take care of you."

"Family? What family?" Talia tried to sit up, but wasn't able to get in a comfortable position. She reached back and rearranged the pillow so she was propped up a bit more. "The only real family I have is Sam, Jacob, and now Kelly. And since most of them are here, I'm staying. Besides, what gives you the right to dictate what I do or where I go?"

"You gave me the right a long time ago, Talia." Megan took hold of her hand in a tight grip. "You promised yourself to me years ago. I mean to keep you to that promise."

"Get the hell out of here." Talia tried to pull away, but Megan's grip was strong. "I mean it. Either leave or I'll call for security to remove you."

"You wouldn't dare." Megan lowered her voice. "We're not going through this again, are we? Your mother and I have decided, and that's that."

"Okay, guess we are going to go through this again, even though I wish we didn't have to." Talia pressed the button for the nurse's station. "I'm done with you, Megan. Let go of my hand and get the hell out of here and out of my life."

Megan took a deep breath, and Talia knew she was about to be treated to another chapter of the Book of Megan's Bizarre Bullshit.

"Can I help you?" The nurse's voice interrupted whatever Megan was about to say.

Talia waited, holding her breath until Megan released her hand and walked out of the room. The cold stare she received made her shiver.

The nurse watched, a knowing look on her face, then met Talia's gaze.

"I'm sorry, Jody. Looks like the problem resolved itself. Thank you." She settled back against the pillows and closed her eyes.

RUBY FRUITS WAS the only lesbian bar left that Kelly would go to. Most of the other bars were what she liked to call "meat markets," and she had long ago decided she didn't need that scene anymore. Not that she could pick up any woman she wanted, but Kelly had no desire to head into another relationship, temporary or permanent. At least not for a while.

It was still early in the evening, and Ruby Fruits was nearly empty. The interior of the bar was decorated with tasteful art ranging from prints by Frido Kahlo to murals of Georgia O'Keeffe's work to the paintings of local artists. The theme, of course, being naked women. Kelly always found herself drawn to the two-seat round table below one of the few pieces of art created by a man, a cheap poster copy of Van Gogh's original, "Nude Woman Reclining." The nude woman lay on her side, with her back to the artist, her long brown hair in a tight braid hanging loosely near her shoulders. What Kelly liked most about the painting was that the woman wasn't one of those bone thin models you often see in modern art. She had flesh on her. A real woman.

She could almost feel the soft curves of her and would love to be able to snuggle against her in that bed.

A voice behind her said, "One of these days I'm going to find out you stole that damn picture."

Kelly tore her eyes away from the Van Gogh, not surprised that her ex, Janine, was joining her. "I just might do that. Maybe I'll even find the chick and take her home."

Janine slid a beer across the table. "I wouldn't be surprised if you did. So, long shift? You haven't been coming in here lately."

Kelly took a swig of her beer and swallowed. "You could say that."

"Been thinking about my offer?"

"Janine, please. Can we not do this? I thought we were going to be friends."

"Yes. With benefits." Janine leaned back in her chair, balancing on its back legs. "You're a tough bitch, Kelly McCoy."

"I do my best."

"You're gonna make one helluva catch."

"Whatever." Kelly put the beer down and pointed to the painting. "Too bad that chick isn't here. She's only a nice dream."

Janine let the chair fall forward so she could lean across the table and take Kelly's hand. "You keep dreaming and you're going to find that none of the women you end up with are good enough. Sometimes you have to take what you can get."

"I don't want to do that." She squeezed Janine's hand before releasing it. "Seriously. Now please, change the subject?"

"Oh, hell," Janine leaned back in the chair again. "You look like hell. That prick giving you a hard time again?"

"Burke? Some. He's just an asshole. I finally got the captain to move him off my shift. I've got seniority over Burke, which pisses him off even more. So the captain said no problem and moved him."

"Good. Homophobic bastard." Janine raised her beer bottle. "Here's to your captain. He's sure made your life easier now."

"Yes, she did." Kelly laughed at the expression on Janine's face. "And before you ask, she's family. So yeah. It wasn't hard to get that done. But it does suck having to see him every morning, since the shift he was moved to relieves mine."

"Ick. I can't imagine seeing any man every morning." Janine's eyes were no longer looking at Kelly. Kelly glanced toward the bar to find a nice-looking brunette, beer in hand, chatting with the bartender. Suppressing a laugh, Kelly thought that Janine was one of the most transparent horndogs she'd ever met. Didn't take her long to shift her romantic focus at all. Kelly figured all of five minutes might pass before Janine would start working on seeing the brunette's face in the morning.

Janine's chair legs hit the floor hard, and she popped up cheerfully. "Catch you later, Kel."

"Nice catching up with you."

"Yep. No problem," she said vaguely as she strolled toward the bar. She didn't look back. Kelly checked her watch, then nearly laughed out loud three minutes later when Janine had her arm around her target. Another ten minutes and they were out the door.

Kelly finished her beer and was ready to leave when her cell phone rang. She didn't recognize the number. "Hello?"

"Kelly? It's Talia."

"Oh hey. How you doing?"

"Completely bored. Just thought I'd call and talk to a friendly person. My nurse has the personality of sand paper."

"I'm not surprised. You can't get all the good nurses without the occasional bad one mixed in."

"I guess so." She paused and Kelly wondered if they'd been disconnected. "Are you busy?"

"Nope." Kelly glanced at her watch. It wasn't quite seven p.m. "Just hanging out."

"That sounds like fun."

Kelly sensed where Talia was going. "You up for a visit? I can be there in about fifteen minutes. And I'm sure I can con Nurse Sand Paper into letting me stay past eight."

"That'd be awesome. If you're sure you're not busy."

Kelly could almost hear the smile in Talia's voice. "I'll be there soon."

THE HOSPITAL ROOM was dark when Kelly arrived, a bouquet of carnations in her hand. She paused in the doorway, wondering if Talia was asleep.

"You can come in. I'm just sitting in the dark." Talia turned on the light above her bed. The fluorescent glow made Kelly blink to adjust her eyes. When she got closer, she saw that Talia had been crying.

"I brought you some fresh flowers." She pulled the wilted ones, dropped them in the trash, and put the new bouquet in the vase. She asked, "You okay?"

"Not really."

"Want to talk about it?" Kelly offered her the box of tissues from the bedside stand.

Talia dried her face and blew her nose. "I don't know. I just needed some company."

"That's why I came here." Kelly ached to know what was bothering her, but didn't want to push Talia. It was enough that she'd called her over. Talia's hands rested in her lap and Kelly placed her hand over them.

Talia's shoulders shook as she sobbed.

Kelly settled on the bed, wrapped her arms around her, and let Talia cry herself to sleep.

WHEN TALIA AWOKE the next morning, the first thing she saw was the vase of carnations and a note on her bedside table. She remembered how shyly Kelly gave her the flowers and the way it felt for Kelly to cradle her in her arms while she cried. She picked up the note.

Talia, I stayed with you until the nurse finally kicked me out. I hope you're doing better after a good night of rest. Please give me a call later.
Hugs,
Kelly

"Oh, how sweet," Talia said aloud and held the note to her chest. She imagined the feel of Kelly's strong arms around her and realized it was the first time she'd felt safe in years. She felt like she belonged in Kelly's arms.

But that was silly. Kelly was just being kind and comforting, nothing more. Though it didn't diminish how much Talia had enjoyed the time. Too bad she'd fallen asleep. It would have been nice to enjoy it for while longer.

"Why didn't you tell me Megan came here?" Jacob said the second he stepped into Talia's room.

"Um, hi, Jacob. It's nice to see you. I'm fine. You?"

"Un-funny."

"Sorry. Just thought I'd get a hello in before I got an ass chewing."

Jacob sat on the corner of Talia's bed and sighed dramatically. "Hello, Talia. Now tell me why you never called me."

"How'd you find out she was here?"

"No questions before you answer mine."

"Because I handled it."

"Did you? Did you know your mother was at your apartment packing things up?"

"What?"

"I already took care of it. I told your apartment manager I'm your lawyer and no one goes in without you or I saying they can.

And nothing comes out, either."

"What the hell? She has no right—"

"Correct. But Megan told her you were merely being stubborn and that you'd be okay with the move once you got settled again in DC."

"And she believed her?" Talia asked. The look on Jacob's face reminded her how rhetorical the question was. "Of course she did. She always believed her over me. I wish she'd just adopt Megan and get it over with. She's the daughter my mother always wanted."

"I know, sweetie. Look. I can have another talk with Megan, if you want me to."

"No, but thanks. I'll talk to Mother."

"I'll get Dylan to go to your place with me and get your stuff put away."

"Dylan? Dylan, your new assistant?"

"The very same."

"Jacob Meier. I thought we had this talk already."

"We did. But that was Joseph and he wasn't my assistant. He was yours," Jacob said, obviously unrepentant.

"Uh huh. Just don't get him pissed off. I don't want to go through that mess again."

"Pfft. Won't happen. We're the happily non-dating-good-sex kind of friends. That's it."

"Nice. Too much information, but nice."

"Speaking of sex, what's the latest on that little hottie, Kelly?"

"There is no latest."

"Yeah." Jacob patted her on the head. "I've seen her look at you, sweetie. You just keep that little un-fantasy in your head. She'll make her move soon enough."

"Jacob—"

"I've got places to go and a little Dylan to make happy." He ignored her continued protests, kissed Talia and left.

Out in the hall, Talia heard Jacob's voice. "You've got timing!" he said, just loud enough for Talia to hear his every word. "Go pull the pouty little princess out of her dark, ugly hole, will you?"

"Sure thing," Kelly said as she walked into the room. She had a strange look on her face and it made Talia laugh. "He's a nice guy. Weird, but nice."

"No kidding. I didn't expect you this morning."

"I just got back from a call."

"I thought you were off last night."

"I was. But there was another big fire and they did a call out. It means that any off duty crews need to come help. So since I wasn't busy I went. Not my favorite way to spend Friday night, but there you have it." Kelly yawned and sank into a chair. "Sorry, but I've only had about an hour of sleep."

"I don't see how you do it." Talia wanted to smooth the unruly red bangs off Kelly's face, but didn't dare.

"You just get used to it, I guess. My dad never got more than a few hours of sleep, even when he wasn't working."

"That must have been hard on you and your mom. Did you get to see him much?"

"He was there for most of my games. I don't know how he did it, but he managed to be there for all of my birthday parties." Kelly's eyes took on a distant look. "Proudest day of my life was when he was there at my graduation from the fire academy. It was so cool to see the expression on his face."

"He must have been proud."

"He was." Kelly cleared her throat.

Talia had no idea what else to say. She never paid much attention to the police officers, EMT's and others that came in and out of the office in DC. Her company there handled insurance contracts for a lot of public safety departments. She hadn't realized how special those people were. The sacrifices they made, the pride they had in their professions...it was almost overwhelming.

She wanted to comment, but Kelly changed the subject.

Chapter
Eleven

KELLY GOT HOME later in the day than she'd planned. Her nap in Talia's room had lasted more than a few hours, but she was glad for the rest. At least she'd remembered to tell her mother where she was going to be.

She made it two feet into the living room before her mother popped up and pulled her onto the couch. She placed a larger envelope on Kelly's lap and said, "We need to talk about our vacation."

"What's this?"

"Our cruise information. We leave in two weeks. Remember?"

"Of course I do." Kelly glanced inside the envelope. How had she forgotten about the cruise she and her mother had been planning all year? With the stress at work, the timing was perfect. But what about Talia?

As if she could read Kelly's thoughts, Marina said, "She'll be fine for a few days without you. I know you well enough to know what you're thinking."

"And what's that?" Kelly folded her arms across her chest.

"You don't want to abandon Talia. You're getting close to her and you're afraid that if you leave she'll be upset." Marina held Kelly's hand. "Which is why you tell her where we're going, make sure she has your cell phone number, and promise to visit when we get back."

"I don't know—"

"We both need this trip, honey. You know that."

"I do." Kelly looked at the package in her lap. "I'll make sure she knows how to reach me."

Marina kissed her on the forehead. "Believe me, if she can wait for you for a week, she's a keeper."

Kelly laughed out loud. "You really think I'm that far gone?"

Marina raised her eyebrow again. "And you don't?"

"Ha ha." Kelly handed her the packet and got up. "I'll be home tonight after class. I'm only scheduled to teach the afternoon part. I'm going to visit Talia first."

Marina slapped Kelly playfully on the thigh as she walked away. "And you have to ask me if you're that far gone. Ha!"

"TALIA?" COLETTE CALLED out as she entered Talia's hospital room. "Are you awake, dear?"

"Yes, Mother. You can come on in." Talia was staring at her cell phone.

"I brought someone I want you to meet."

Talia stared at the man her mother was ushering into the room. He was a tall, light-skinned black man with a tan suit that didn't look very good on him. "Who's that?" Talia pressed the button to raise her bed so she was sitting up.

"I'm Delmar Clark, the attorney hired to represent you."

"An attorney?" Talia asked, looking to Colette. "Why do I need an attorney?"

"He's handling the lawsuit, Talia."

"What lawsuit?"

"The one against James Robert Colwell." Colette sat daintily in the chair Delmar Clark pulled out for her while he remained standing by her side. "It's been a week, so we need to get moving on this."

"I don't know anyone named James Colwell. Who is he and why are you suing him?"

"You're suing him," Delmar said. He handed a folder to Talia. "I've got all the papers drawn up. We just need you to sign, and I'll get this to the courthouse today."

"Wait, wait, wait. I'm not signing a damn thing. Who is James Colwell?"

"The man driving the truck," Colette said. "He's the one who hurt you, and we're going to make sure you get compensated. I'm sure the man had insurance."

"Mother. The man died in the accident. You can't sue a dead man."

Talia didn't like the look that crossed Delmar Clark's face. "We're not suing him. We're suing his family. They're culpable for anything he did."

"Not a chance in hell." Talia tried to rip the folder in half, but didn't have the strength. She took a few of the papers out and quickly ripped them to small pieces. "You won't sue anyone, Mother. That man's family has gone through enough. He died and hurt a lot of people in the process, but I'm not holding his family responsible."

"Talia, be reasonable. He ruined your life. If you lose your leg—"

"I'll deal with that when and if it happens. But I won't ruin someone else's life along the way. Mother, I can't believe you'd be this callous."

"She's being reasonable," Delmar Clark said. "You deserve the money."

Talia threw the paper pieces at him. "I don't want it. Now get the hell out of here."

"Talia, please. Mr. Clark is a top-rate lawyer."

"Mother, if anything is done legally, I will deal with it through Jacob. He's working with our company to make sure I get paid while I'm in here and to make sure my medical bills are covered. That's enough for me."

"Then I suppose we're done here. Colette, I'll be in touch." Delmar Clark left the room without another word.

"Talia, why were you so rude to him? He's only trying to help us."

"Why didn't you talk to me before you called him? You know Jacob's a lawyer. Doesn't it make sense that he'd help me? He is my best friend after all."

"I realize that. I just wanted you to have the best."

"I already do."

"If you're referring to that Jacob Meier, I wouldn't consider him the best. He showed up at your apartment last night and ordered me to stop packing."

"Because I asked him to." Talia turned away from her. "I'm not leaving and you shouldn't have started packing my stuff."

"I was trying to help you."

"I know. Look, I'm tired. I think I need to rest."

"Of course, dear. I'll see you tomorrow."

"SO HOW'S MY favorite patient this morning?" Kelly leaned against the rail of Talia's bed and smiled at the cranky look on her new friend's face. "Oh, not a morning person?"

"And you are?"

Kelly laughed. "Actually, I am. But only after I've had at least three cups of solid black coffee to bring my body to life."

Talia yawned and stretched both arms in the air. "Same here. Got any of that coffee on ya?"

Kelly held up a white bag with a Starbucks label. "As a matter of fact, I do."

"Oh, I love you!" Talia used the controls to raise the bed so she could take the tall cardboard container and sip at the hot brew. "Heavenly."

"Wow. I guess it's been a while since you've had any real coffee."

"How can you tell?"

"Because you're holding that with both hands and sucking it down like there's no tomorrow. Guess you needed some caffeine."

"You better believe it." Talia rested the cup on her stomach. "My ex-partner used to set the coffeemaker for 5 a.m. so I'd have fresh brew every morning." Talia scoffed, "It was the only nice thing she ever did for me."

"How long were you together?"

"Ten years too long." Talia took another sip and sighed contentedly. "Megan was controlling and thanks to Jacob I got out of that relationship. That's why I took a job out here."

"Stupid woman to let you go like that."

"Oh, she wanted to keep me. She was more than willing to take and take, while I gave."

"That sucks."

"It did. But I kicked her out of my house about two years ago. She kept coming around wanting money until finally I sold my house and escaped here. She's a corporate lawyer with a shopping habit to rival Paris Hilton. Last I heard she was living with some friends, but I'd lost track of her."

"Sounds like a good thing." Kelly settled into the chair beside the bed. "My girlfriend left me when I refused to kick my mother out of the house so she could live with me alone."

"Bitch. Does your mother have a problem with you having a girlfriend?"

"Nope. My girlfriend had a problem with me having a mother." Kelly leaned back in the chair and rested her feet on the edge of Talia's bed. "Ma works nights, and I don't want her living alone. Besides, we found a house that was affordable and large enough that she's got her side and I have mine. She's more like a roommate than anything else."

"Sounds like you two have a good arrangement."

"It works for us. We're all the family we have."

Talia handed her the empty cup. "Thanks. You're a saint."

"Hardly." Kelly tossed it into a trash can. "How you feeling today?"

"Sore, but okay. My leg is hurting more than anything."

"Mind if I take a look?"

Talia shook her head and Kelly moved the covers back. They had bandaged her right leg past the knee and her toes were an odd bluish color. The leg was losing circulation.

"How bad is it, Doctor McCoy?"

"It's wrapped up in bandages so I can't see it. Little bit of bruising around the packaging. But I've heard of that orthopedic doc they gave you. She's a doc for the Bengals football team."

"The look on your face doesn't sound as hopeful as your voice."

Kelly tried to smile. "I'm not a doctor, but I play one on TV."

"Smart ass."

"Better a smart ass than a dumb ass."

"As long as you get a little ass, it's all good." Both women giggled at their silly conversation.

"Before I forget," Kelly reached into her pocket and handed Talia a slip of paper. "Ma and I are going on a cruise Thursday, and we won't be back until next Tuesday. But you can call me any time you like."

"A cruise?" Talia's eyes lit up. "Where to?"

"The Caribbean. It's gonna be cool because neither of us has ever been out of the country."

"You'll love it. Megan and I went on a cruise. It was wonderfully relaxing and an amazing time. You'll hate having to come home."

"Really?" Kelly watched the excitement in Talia's eyes. "I guess I'm looking forward to this trip then."

"You weren't before?"

"Not so much." Kelly shrugged. "To be honest, I don't want to leave you." Kelly felt a strange tugging in her stomach. Oh, geez, she thought. That was so lame.

"Why?"

"Sounds dumb, huh?"

"No. I think it's sweet." She touched the side of Kelly's face. The gesture warmed Kelly's skin and settled her nerves.

"Just being honest," Kelly said. "I won't be able to bring you coffee from the ocean."

"That's fine." Talia waved her hand in the air. "I can con Jacob into being my cabana boy while you're gone. It'll be fun to make him bring me coffee every morning."

"He's a sweet guy."

"He's the best friend I've ever had. But you come in a close second."

"And after just a couple of weeks? Thanks." Kelly leaned on the adjustable table beside Talia's bed and knocked a large manila envelope to the ground. "Oops. Sorry 'bout that." She bent to pick it up and glanced at the label on the front. "Delmar Clark? The attorney?"

Talia sighed. "Yes. The lawyer my mother hired for her lawsuit."

"Who's she suing?"

"No one." Talia closed her eyes and scrubbed her face with one hand. "My mother decided I should sue the poor guy driving the truck that hit me."

"Why would she sue a dead man? She's not getting any money out of him."

"I like your logic, but he probably had life insurance and his family could be sued, maybe some of his assets taken away. But I'm not about to do that. His car insurance company is probably duking things out, and when the dust settles, I expect things will work out. I don't even want to know why he did what he did." Talia reached for Kelly's hand. "I told Mother and Mr. Clark I have no intention of suing anyone. I'm just glad I survived."

"That's your choice," Kelly said. She squeezed Talia's hand. "But you're probably the only one. There're family members of the others who died and those who got hurt who will probably sue his family. I feel sorry for them. It's not right to make his family responsible for what he did."

"No, it's not. So, can we talk about something else?"

"I'd love to, but I need to get a few hours of sleep before tonight. I've got a class to teach."

"Teach? You're a firefighter, paramedic, and a teacher?"

"I teach ACLS—Advanced Cardiac Life Support—it's basically CPR with drugs. And I've got to be at the hospital at six tonight."

"Wow, you're a busy woman. When do you find time for a social life?"

Kelly laughed and stood. "Social life? What's that?"

"Ah. Point taken."

"I'll stop by tomorrow morning."

"Bring coffee."

Chapter
Twelve

TALIA SHOVED THE breakfast tray away, unable to stomach the stuff the hospital called food. She flipped open her cell phone to call Jacob and was pleasantly surprised when he walked in.

"Timing is as good as ever."

"Isn't it always?" he said, holding up a brown paper bag.

"If that contains something resembling food, I will love you forever."

"You'll love me anyway, but yes. One blueberry bagel coming up." He removed the food tray from her bed table and placed the paper bag there.

Talia let out a little squeal when she found a Styrofoam cup of steaming coffee. "I love you."

"Yes. We already established that. So, do you want to hear how brilliant I am?"

"You were born brilliant," Talia said around bites of her breakfast. "But I'm sure there's more to tell."

"I spoke with the owners of your office building today, along with their lawyer, who just happened to be in my fraternity. We worked out a financial settlement, and my assistant will have it all ready for you to review by lunchtime."

"Excellent work, Mr. Meier. Please, do tell me the details."

"I'll sum it up. They're paying whatever hospital bills aren't covered by the various insurances of those found responsible, and of course, the expenses you may incur in later years from all this will also be paid. They've offered you a tidy sum for your pain and suffering—six figures."

"Jacob, this is great. Are you sure that Mr. Colwell's family isn't going to be brought into all this?"

"Here is where my brilliance shines best. He didn't have a family to speak of. So far, I'm the only lawyer that's come to the building owners for compensation. Now, this is still in negotiations, but I'm confident we'll have it closed by the end of next week."

"How did you manage all of this? It wasn't the owner of the building's fault that guy ran his truck through the atrium."

"Actually, it sort of was. He was terminally ill, and our company denied an insurance claim for some last-ditch medical procedures he thought he needed. I didn't get all the details, but he left a note in the truck saying if he was going to die, he'd do it on his own terms."

"So our own company is paying all my bills?"

"Yours and anyone else who was hurt. The company is trying to avoid any lawsuits by paying everyone off, basically. Since you're an employee, we came to an agreement so you could be taken care of, and you'll get your normal salary until you're ready to go back to work."

"Remind me to hire you as my lawyer some time."

Jacob buffed his fingers on his shirt. "Honey, you can't afford me."

"Whatever. Thanks for taking care of all this, Jacob. Seriously."

"Of course. For you, it's pro bono. Unless you've got some chocolate lying around here somewhere?"

"Sadly, there's none left. But I have another project for you. Please call Delmar Clark and make sure my mother's ridiculous law suit was actually stopped."

Jacob rolled his eyes. "He's an ambulance-chasing bastard. I have his number at the office. I need to head there anyway. I'll call him. Promise to get some rest."

"Yes, dear."

"And tell Kelly I said hello."

"I will if she calls me." Talia glanced at her cell phone and Jacob paused in the doorway.

"She hasn't phoned you today?"

"No." Talia flipped open her phone just to make sure there were no calls missed. "She and her mother are leaving for Miami tomorrow morning. I was hoping to hear from her, but I guess she's too busy getting ready to go. She said she'd try to get hold of me once they were either at the airport or aboard ship."

"I'm sure she'll catch up with you soon, sweetie. When does she return?"

"She said she'd be home on Tuesday to meet Daddy when he comes to visit after his business trip."

"Women," Jacob sighed dramatically. "Honey, you'll hear from her. She's called ten times a day for the last two weeks."

"I'm sure you're right."

"I'm always right." Jacob blew her a kiss. "You find me if you need me."

"Don't I always?"

HER MOTHER'S VOICE droned on and on and sounded like the teacher's voice from *Peanuts*. Talia stared at the stark white walls of her room, wishing that Kelly would call and wondering if her mother was ever going to leave her alone.

"Aaron won't be coming," Colette said.

"Why not?" Talia asked, figuring she'd better comment so her mother wouldn't yell at her for not listening.

"Little Dina has the flu, and Sheila can't take off work to stay home with her."

"Of course. How convenient," Talia muttered. It was so typical of Aaron to find a reason not to come. He'd spent most of his youth fine-tuning the art of disappointing them. Why would his adulthood be any different?

"He did say he'd try to get another flight next week. He wants to see you."

"Yippie." Talia held up her hand to stop her mother's retort. "Let's not fight about Aaron. I don't feel like arguing."

"Fine. Though I don't understand why you don't like him. He's your brother."

"I love him as my brother because we're genetically attached. But that's it. Please, Mother."

Colette was silent for a moment. "Has your father been by to see you?"

So much for not arguing. "Yes. He came by last night and said he'd be here this evening. He also wants to meet Kelly, and she said she'd stop by on Tuesday so he's going to stay a few days in Cincinnati."

"Why would he want to meet her?"

"To thank her for saving my life."

"You can't be serious." Colette crossed her arms and huffed.

"I am and he is. Kelly was there in that hellhole of debris with me the entire time. She risked her life and did more for me than you realize. I wish you'd be nicer to her. She's very sweet."

"She may be sweet, dear, but I don't like you associating with her."

"Why?"

"You know why."

"Because she's gay? I thought you got over that with Megan."

"I'll never 'get over it' as you so bluntly put it." Colette held up a hand to stop Talia's response. "However, Megan was, and still is, a fine match for you. She comes from an up-standing family, she's well-mannered, and she still cares deeply for you."

"Megan cares about Megan. I'm just sorry you can't see that. I know she's the perfect daughter for you, but you need to understand that Kelly is my friend, and I'm not going to push her away because she doesn't come from some upper class, snooty family."

"Uh oh," Sam said from the doorway, frozen in place. "Should I let you two have this fight and come back later?"

"Samuel Stoddard, get in here," Colette said. "I really wish you could talk some sense into your sister."

"That's a good one. Little T hasn't had sense since, well, I don't think she's ever had good sense."

"I'd hit you if you were closer to the bed." Talia shook her fist at him, but it made Sam laugh more. "I'm not so little anymore, you know?"

"Ah, always dreaming of kicking my ass." Sam stood just out of her reach. "Someday, kid, you just might."

"When you're not expecting it."

"Stop it, you two." Colette pointed toward a chair. "Sam, sit down and behave."

"Sorry, I can't." He turned a serious gaze to Talia. "My unit is being deployed, and since you're no longer in danger of dying, my leave is canceled."

"No, Sam." Talia held her arms out and hugged him tightly. "I hate it when you go off to fight."

"I know. But it's my job, T. Don't worry. I'll be okay." He kissed her on the forehead and turned to their mother. "Sorry for the short notice."

"I understand." Colette rose to hug him. "Be careful, son. And remember how proud I am of you."

"I will. My flight leaves in an hour, so I have to get going." He stood ramrod straight and saluted them properly. "I love you both, and I'll write as soon as I can." He tossed a plastic bag at Talia and grinned. "Just something to keep you company."

She pulled a teddy bear from the bag. The bear was dressed in military camouflage and had captain's bars pinned to the collar. Tears filled Talia's eyes, and she held the bear close to her heart. When she looked up, Sam was already gone.

Chapter
Thirteen

THE FANFARE OF the cruise ship leaving port had been a bit much for Kelly. She was ready to sit back and relax, but her mother was off and running. The confetti and streamers hadn't even settled on deck before Marina found a Bingo game, and knowing her mother, it would be cutthroat Bingo. God help anyone that beat her.

Kelly dipped her feet into warm, clear pool water and wiggled her toes. She leaned back and enjoyed the feel of the sun on her face. Kelly sensed, rather than saw, a woman sit down beside her.

"Amazing view, huh?" the woman asked.

Kelly followed her gaze. The sun was setting on the horizon. She hadn't realized how late it was. The orange and yellow hues reflecting off the water seemed to go on forever. It was a pretty sight and she nodded her head in agreement. "Yep. Don't get views like that back home."

"Where's home?"

"Cincinnati. You?"

"Middletown," she said with a lot of enthusiasm. "Wow. We're practically neighbors. Where in Cincinnati do you live?"

Kelly turned slightly and eyed her for a moment. She didn't look familiar, but plenty of her was on display. She wore a string bikini that left nothing to the imagination. "Not far from downtown."

She smiled at Kelly with a set of perfect, white teeth. "Small world."

"Yeah." Kelly felt appraising eyes on her and was suddenly uncomfortable. "I should —"

"I'm Annie Spiner." She held out her hand and Kelly awkwardly shook it.

"Kelly," she said hesitantly, not bothering to give the woman her last name. She had a feeling this woman wouldn't care to know it.

"Would you like to take a walk, Kelly? I was thinking of going back to my stateroom for a drink." She flashed her smile again. "I'd love for you to join me."

Oh, yeah. She was getting the right vibes. "Nah. I need to find my mom and make sure she eats dinner. She gets so caught up in playing Bingo that she doesn't know when to stop." She lied easily, knowing well her mother would never miss a meal and could be counted on to track Kelly down in an hour.

"Hmm. How 'bout we meet later tonight?" She scooted close enough to Kelly that the bare skin of their shoulders touched.

Annie was gorgeous, and a few weeks ago, her offer would have tempted Kelly, but not now. Dark eyes, smooth brown skin, and long black hair that Kelly ached to tangle her fingers in were all she could think about. Any time she closed her eyes she easily conjured up Talia's face, heard her voice, and little thrills raced through her body. She had never been this attracted to Janine.

And she certainly wasn't attracted to the woman sitting beside her. Kelly slid into the warm water and looked back at Annie. "Sorry. I'm busy."

"You don't look busy." Annie followed her into the pool and treaded water until she was inches from Kelly. "You look amazing."

Kelly didn't like the way Annie's eyes raked over her body, as if she were new candy to be tasted. She wished that a different pair of eyes were looking at her with that kind of desire. In her mind Talia treaded in front of her, hair slicked back from her face. Her full body within inches of Kelly's hands. She imagined caressing her ample breasts, her hands sliding down the curves of Talia's body...

But Annie wasn't Talia. Kelly said, "Seriously. I'm not interested."

"But I'm not wrong about you, am I?" Annie asked, reaching her hand out to lightly caress Kelly's breasts.

"Oh no." Kelly moved away. She knew she didn't want anything to do with Annie, but her body betrayed her. "I mean, yeah. I'm gay, but no, I don't want to be with you."

"Really?" Annie looked hurt and Kelly backpedaled.

"Let me try this again. Yes, I'm gay. Yes, you're beautiful, but I'm taken." Kelly surprised herself as well as Annie by her remark.

"Taken? I don't see a ring."

"We're just not there yet." Not quite the truth, but this time she didn't feel like she was lying. Neither she nor Talia had made any promises to each other. They hadn't done much more than chat. They'd shared a few promising touches, yet Kelly felt deeply attached her. Attached in the way one is attached to her soulmate. "I'm sorry if I led you on."

Annie shook her head. "Are you sure you don't want to at least have dinner with me?"

"I can't." Kelly moved to the steps and got out of the pool. "Have a fun cruise."

"Yeah." Annie frowned. "Fun." With short choppy, strokes, she swam to the other end of the pool.

Kelly stood there long enough to watch Annie make a move on

another woman before walking off to find her Bingo-addict mother and some dinner.

KELLY LEANED ON the deck rail and gazed out at the clear night sky. A city kid all her life, it was a rare treat to see all the bright lights in the horizon. She still held her cell phone in her left hand hoping for the off chance that she could get a signal from the deck. The phone was still searching for a tower. Kelly wanted to throw the damn thing into the Atlantic Ocean.

Talia had been on her mind since earlier in the day when that Annie person hit on her. Kelly needed to hear Talia's voice. She'd heard her recorded voice several times since getting on the airplane to Miami. Talia's voicemail had not been very soothing. She wanted to talk to a real live Talia.

She looked at her cell phone again. Jacob had stopped by the day before she and Ma left for Miami. He'd made it a point to come to Kelly's house and ask her to call Talia. That seemed a little weird, since Kelly hardly knew the guy. But he'd been insistent.

Kelly reassured him that she didn't intend to be gone for five days without calling Talia. She remembered Jacob saying something like, "She's a little skittish. You didn't call yesterday so she thinks maybe you don't want to see her."

"But I did call," Kelly said. "All I got was a message that her voice mail box is full."

"She's horrible about deleting voice mail. Look, I'll get her to clear out her inbox. Just call her, okay?"

Kelly had agreed and watched Talia's best friend climb into his car and leave.

That was two days ago.

Since then it had been one thing after the other, barely making it to the airport, their hotel reservations messed up, arriving at the ship just before it left. Kelly had scarcely had time to breathe, but her thoughts were on Talia. It would be enough to hear Talia's voice and say good night. Though it would be better to have Talia at her side to enjoy the sunset.

The phone blinked indicating it was still searching for a tower. Kelly cursed under her breath and was ready to turn the thing off when it beeped twice. Finally, a signal.

Kelly flipped open her phone and hit the "send" button. The phone rang a few times and went to voice mail.

"Hi, Talia. It's Kelly. Look, I haven't had a chance to call you yet and this is the first time I've had a signal. Call me as soon as you get this message." She closed her phone and stared out at the stars again.

Something wasn't right. She was in the same time zone as Ohio, and Talia should be getting finished with her dinner. Why hadn't she answered the phone?

Kelly decided to call her again, in case Talia had been talking to someone else at the time she called. Again, the call went to voice mail. "Hey, it's me. I hate talking to a machine, but I really want to hear your voice. Does that sound lame? Call me. Please."

Kelly closed the phone and cursed herself. She sounded pathetic and desperate. She dialed Talia's number. "Me again. You're very important to me, Talia. And this is too important to leave as a message on your voice mail. So call me on my cell. Please?"

She hung up again and this time tucked the phone into her jacket pocket.

Kelly continued to lean on the rail until the evening chill got to her. Deciding to head back, she took the phone out one last time and strolled toward her quarters. She almost dropped it when it rang. She flipped it open without looking to see who the caller was. "Hello?"

"Hi."

It was wonderful to hear Talia's voice. Kelly had trouble forming any words. "Hey."

An awkward silence fell, and Kelly stepped into her stateroom, closing the door behind her. "I've been trying to get a hold of you."

"Yeah. My phone got set to silence, and I didn't realize it." Talia hesitated and Kelly heard her moving around on the bed. "I did listen to your voicemails, though."

"Good. Jacob said you were bad about clearing those out."

Talia laughed. "I am. But when I saw that it was your number I was afraid to listen to them."

"Afraid? Why would you be afraid?" Kelly sat on her bed.

"You didn't call me Wednesday or Thursday and — and I needed you. I couldn't reach you, and I just figured you weren't interested anymore."

"Talia, I haven't stopped thinking about you since the day I left your hospital room. I've been going nuts trying to reach you."

"I'm — I'm sorry."

Was she crying? Kelly thought she heard a sob. "Please. I'm not angry. Don't be upset." She leaned back on the bed, wishing more than anything that she could be next to Talia. Wishing she could give her a kiss. "Don't cry, baby. I got a little worried. That's all."

"I didn't think you wanted anything to do with me." Talia said. "I honestly thought you were gently telling me to go away."

"Hell no." Kelly closed her eyes and imagined Talia beside her, holding her hand. "I'd never do that. Didn't you hear me before? You're all I've been able to think about."

"Seriously?" She heard a hitch in Talia's voice.

"Since the day I first met you." There was another awkward pause.

Talia said, "I've been thinking of you a lot, too."

"Great minds think alike," Kelly said, elated to hear Talia's soft chuckle. She got up from the bed and looked out the porthole. Millions of tiny points of light filled the inky blackness above. "I wanted to share the evening sky with you."

"You did?" Did she hear apprehension in Talia's voice? Or surprise?

"Of course. It's not as much fun looking at it alone. Besides, I find it terribly romantic. I should have warned you that I'm a mushball for romance."

"I like that. I've never been much on romance. Then again, I've never had a reason to be."

"Then I'll have to give you a reason."

A comfortable silence settled over both of them. Talia was the first to speak again. "I've got surgery Monday morning. The doctor didn't sound too optimistic about saving my leg." Talia paused and Kelly waited for her to continue. "Maybe you could call me at sunset and describe how it looks."

"I'd love to share it with you. Tonight's was pretty amazing." She went on to describe the skies, ship, the pool, and the astounding array of food at the dinner banquet. They talked effortlessly, as though they'd known each other for years, until finally Kelly could tell Talia was starting to fade. "I bet you had some meds recently."

"Yeah, sorry. After a while, they make me fuzzy."

"I'll let you go then, and I'll try to call again tomorrow. I hope I can get a signal. I've got plenty more stories to tell you."

"I'd love to hear them." She yawned in the background, which made Kelly smile.

"Please try not to worry too much about the surgery. I'll be there with you in spirit, holding your hand."

"Thanks. That means a lot to me. Good night, Kelly."

"Good night, Talia." Kelly flipped the phone shut and felt like crying. What had she done to make Talia think she didn't want to be around her? Had she said something? She'd tried to call, but Talia obviously didn't know that. And what about her surgery? Kelly would give anything to have a helicopter pick her up and take her off the damn ship.

"It's about time you called her." Marina appeared in the doorway and startled Kelly.

"How long have you been standing there?"

"Long enough." Marina flopped onto Kelly's bed. "So, how is she doing?"

"She's okay, I think." Kelly highlighted their conversation. "I wish I could be there for her."

"Just think good thoughts." Marina said. She put her arm around Kelly's shoulders and gave her a squeeze. "No crying. Nothing bad has happened so far, and you're not allowed to think negative thoughts."

Kelly swiped the tears from her cheeks. "Okay. Even if she loses the leg, she's still alive and well."

"And still interested in you, right? After all, she wouldn't be upset that you didn't call if she wasn't interested."

Kelly eyed her mother suspiciously. "Oh, no. You're not getting the whole conversation out of me."

"Why not? I'm your mother. You should be a good daughter and share these things with me."

"I'm a good daughter, but I'm not sharing." Kelly shoved the phone into her pocket. "But I will go with you to the casino."

"And you're buying me a beer."

"You don't drink." Kelly said as she opened the door of their stateroom.

"I do when I gamble."

"Since when?"

"Since I'm on a cruise and I can."

Kelly fell into step behind her.

"And don't you roll your eyes at me, young lady."

"How did—"

"I'm your mother."

Chapter
Fourteen

THE SOUND OF loud music startled Talia awake, and she fumbled about, hunting for her cell phone on the bedside table.

"Hello?"

"Hi." Kelly said. She sounded distracted.

Talia rubbed her eyes to try to wake herself up. "Hey, Kelly. What are you up to?"

"Hmm, nothing much." Kelly paused and Talia waited out the silence. "I'm just missing you."

"Really? Well that's funny, because I'm missing you right now." Talia felt her face flush with heat. She felt like a teenager talking to her first crush.

"We make quite a pair, don't we?" Kelly chuckled, and the sound made Talia laugh, too.

"Sure do. Are you having a good time?"

"Oh, yeah. Mom has been either playing Bingo or at the slot machines every waking moment, except when I made her leave the ship to go on an island tour today."

"Did she enjoy the tour?"

"Yep, but couldn't wait to get back and play more Bingo. Not only is she addicted, she's on a major winning streak."

"How much?"

"That depends on your math," Kelly said. "My mother's math is messed up. She wins a hundred, plays it back, loses two hundred, wins it back, feeds her money to the slot machine, and then spends her dollars on Bingo and the rip-off tickets. I've never seen her gamble so much in my life."

"Sounds like she's spending your inheritance."

"Hey, yeah. I would be a thousandaire if she'd only stop spending it."

"She's having a good time. What are you doing?"

"I'm getting a tan."

Talia thought for a moment about Kelly in a bikini on a lounge chair soaking up the warm sun, her trim body inches from Talia's reach.

"You still there?"

Whoops. Talia blushed again, glad that Kelly didn't know the contents of her thoughts. "Yeah, I mean no. Guess we must have had a break in our connection or something. What were you saying?"

"I was just saying my tan is more like a sunburn. Redheads don't tan well. Which has nothing to do with the story I wanted to tell you last night. There was this gorgeous woman hitting on me."

Talia felt a twinge in her gut. "Really?" She wanted to ask if Kelly had taken her up on it, but couldn't make herself form the words.

"Yeah. She was pretty bold. I mean, she didn't even know if I was gay or not. It's not like we're on an Olivia Cruise or something. Anyway, she took some swings and struck out."

"She did?" Never much of a sports fan, Talia had trouble processing Kelly's baseball reference. "She struck out?"

"Yeah. As in I said no." Kelly's voice got softer. "I wasn't interested in her, you know."

"Hmm." Talia grinned now, catching on to Kelly's meaning. "Anyone else you're interested in?"

"You bet." Kelly paused, and Talia enjoyed the sound of her breathing. "I need to get going. I'm not sure where Ma is right now, and it's getting close to lunch time."

Talia snuggled beneath her blanket. "I can always sleep more."

"I hear that. What time is your surgery tomorrow?"

"The inhuman hour of six a.m. That's what time I have to be in the pre-op. I don't think the surgeon even gets here until nine. Why do I have to be up if he isn't? I so don't want this surgery."

"I know you don't, baby. But remember I'll be there holding your hand."

Talia felt a flutter in her chest and goose bumps on her arms. "Thanks." It was all she could manage to say. Silence on the other end of the line caused Talia to wonder if she'd lost the connection with Kelly. "What? Are you there?"

"I didn't—I hope you don't mind that I called you baby just now. It kind of slipped out."

"It's okay." It was more than okay. "I liked it."

"Yeah?" Kelly sounded unsure of herself.

"Yeah." Talia said, putting emphasis on the word. "So, you need to find your mom?"

"Oh, I just found her." Kelly said something, but her voice sounded muffled. "She's been standing behind me the whole time. She's a professional eavesdropper, and it's killing her not to hear our conversation."

Talia joined in the laughter. "She should meet my mother. They could trade secrets."

"I bet."

"Now that I've found Ma I best get her to some food."

"Talk to you soon?"

"It's a deal, babe. Bye."

"Bye."

Talia folded her cell phone closed and placed it on the bed next to her hip. Her door opened and a young woman placed a tray on the table beside her bed. Talia tried to hide her disappointment when she lifted the lid on the plate. It looked like eggs, smelled a little like eggs, but she was pretty sure that scrambled eggs weren't supposed to be runny. She sighed and put the lid back on. The food wasn't entirely bad here, but a lot of it wasn't very good either. She wondered if her body would be whittled down to a thin stick by the time they released her. Hospital Weight Loss Program.

"Where's Jacob when I need him?"

Her best friend popped his head into the room. "You rang?"

"If you have a bagel in that bag you're holding I'll give you my firstborn."

Jacob laughed heartily. "Honey, you know damn well neither of us is parenting material." He tossed a small brown bag onto her lap and pulled the food tray away from her. "Eat up. You can put me in your will."

"Oh sure," Talia said between bites of the warm, raisin bagel. "I'll leave you my hundreds of dollars."

"Humph. Might be a bit more than that before too long." Jacob made himself comfortable on the edge of her bed. "So, any word from the cute redhead?"

"Her name is Kelly."

"Any news from Miss Kelly?"

"We just got off the phone."

"Good. I figured if you hadn't heard from her by this evening I'd call her myself."

"And what would you have said to her?"

"I'd have asked her when she's going to ravage you."

"Jacob!"

"Someone's got to pop the question."

"Don't you dare!"

He waved the comment away. "So, is the little hottie enjoying her cruise?"

"Yes, she is." Talia reached into the bag for another bagel. "Stop being so nosy. If anything of importance happens I'll let you know."

"You better. My own life is way too boring. I need to hear about yours so I can live vicariously."

"You want to be in a hospital with a broken leg, not to mention all the internal problems?"

"No." He tapped her good leg playfully. "I want a gorgeous redhead sitting by my side watching my every move and ready to jump on me the moment I snap my fingers." He snapped his fingers to demonstrate. "That's what I want."

"Yeah, me, too." She winked at him and finished off the bagel. "Got any more?"

"Women." He handed her another bag. "Never satisfied."

THE PICKUP AREA at Cincinnati-Northern Kentucky Airport was crowded with people, and Kelly had a tough time finding Scott's truck. She'd called him when they left baggage claim, but with all the traffic she wondered if he'd even see them.

The afternoon sun shone brightly, and the moment Kelly stepped out of the airport, she was smacked in the face by a wave of humidity. "Ick. Can't we go back to the Caribbean?"

Marina said, "Not if you want to see Talia and make sure her surgery went well."

"You sure know how to put reality into a fantasy, Ma."

"Just doing my job."

Kelly spotted Scott and flagged him down. He parked his red Ford F-350, got out, and gave Marina and Kelly hugs. "I don't remember you having so much luggage when you two left," he said as he loaded their belongings into the back of his truck. "And I know they weren't this heavy."

"Sorry you're such a weak and dainty man, Scott." Marina squeezed his bicep and winked at him. "Maybe we ought to call a porter to help you, little fellow."

"Why did I agree to pick you two up?"

"Because you're nice." Kelly tossed in a small gym bag, finishing off their stack of baggage. "Besides, a guy your age has trouble picking up women. All this brute effort and muscle-flexing is good for your image."

"Hmm. When did thirty-nine get old?"

"The same time that fifty-eight did," Marina said.

Scott pretended to inspect his truck tires. "I think the rear is riding kinda low now. I'll have to take your stuff home and come get you two later."

"Scott Sanderson, get in the truck and take us home like a good boy," Marina called from the front passenger seat.

Kelly giggled as Scott obediently got behind the wheel. "Wow. You jump pretty high for her, and she's not even your mother."

"She's a mother. That's enough."

Marina patted him on the head. "Good boy."

Kelly settled into the truck's rear seat and listened to her mother babble about their trip. The cruise had been fun and relaxing, but now she ached to see Talia, and she knew she wouldn't get to until after dinner, now that her mother had asked him to stay.

There had been something tugging at the back of her mind all day. She hadn't heard from Talia after the surgery and had left more messages on her voice mail. She'd even tried to call Jacob, but had to leave messages for him, too. She felt edgy and worried, but tried to put her concerns aside for the time being.

At home, Scott placed the last of the bags in the front hall of the McCoy home and wandered into the kitchen, making a show of sitting heavily into a chair at the table. "I'm beat."

Kelly followed him. "You're the biggest pu — "

"I will wash that mouth out with soap," her mother said, "if you say that word, young lady."

Kelly closed her mouth, and Scott triumphantly stuck his tongue out at her. She said, "Wimp. You didn't have to lug all that stuff across two airports."

"Neither did you," Marina said. "You pushed the cart, Kelly. I hardly count that as 'lugging'."

"I had to load and unload it. A lot." Kelly persisted, smacking the back of Scott's head when he stuck his tongue out again.

"Hey!" Scott said.

"Knock it off you two."

"He started it!"

"She started it!" They broke into laughter.

Marina gathered some food from the cabinets to prepare their dinner . "I raise one child and end up with two. How?"

"Because you're so good with children." Scott rose and kissed her on the forehead. "That's why you adopted me."

"I adopted you under protest." She swatted him with a spatula. "Go get cleaned up. Both of you. I'll not have you eating my food when you're dirty."

"Yes, mom," they chorused and raced each other to the bathroom.

When dinner was finished, Scott helped Kelly with the dishes, then they made their way to the back porch. Kelly kept looking at her watch, hoping Scott would hurry up and leave. She wanted nothing more than to get in the car and race over to the hospital to check on Talia. Instead, she felt she needed to be polite as she listened to him recounting stationhouse politics and recent rescues. After a while, Kelly rose and came back with sodas.

"Hey," he said, "I saw all those beers in the fridge. I'm legal to drink, you know?"

"Yeah, and you're driving home, remember?"

Scott opened the bottle and took a drink. "So, have you talked to Talia since you got back?"

"Scott, you've been with me the whole time I've been home. Have you seen me talking to her?"

"No, but you could have done it before you got to baggage claim at the airport. Or maybe you could have snuck off to the bathroom to call her."

"I don't need to sneak off."

"You do if you don't want your mom to hear your conversation."

"True, but I haven't called. I'm thinking I'll sneak in later and check on her."

Scott reached over and slipped the cell phone from the clip on Kelly's belt. "Here." He handed it to her. "Call. Talk."

"I left her messages earlier. She might be asleep."

"Then call the nurses' station. You can at least find out how she's doing."

Kelly dialed the number and spoke to a nurse. The call was brief and when she closed her cell phone she felt like someone had punched her in the gut. Her face must have given away her feelings, because Scott had hold of her arm and was talking to her.

"Dammit, Kel, tell me what's going on?"

"They took her leg." Her voice sounded distant and flat, like it wasn't coming from her own mouth.

"But didn't you expect that? I thought you said the docs weren't thinking they could save it."

"Yeah, that's what they said. But Talia was so sure it wasn't going to happen. And I wasn't there with her when she woke up. God, Scott, I should have been at her side. And the nurse specifically said no visitors now. Talia is being closely monitored in ICU in wake of the surgery."

"Oh, man, that sucks, Kel." Scott said. "But hang tight. You'll see her first thing in the morning. I'll go with you if you want me to."

Could she feel any worse? And she didn't think she could possibly stop the internal turmoil until she actually saw Talia and assured herself that she was all right. "I think I'd like that. I don't want to run across her mother by myself."

Scott hugged her tightly. "I got your back. You know that."

Kelly extricated herself, went into the kitchen, and came back with a cold beer in hand.

"Hey, that's not fair."

"You have to drive. I, on the other hand, get to stay home now." She took a swig. "Good thing I've got more."

Chapter
Fifteen

THE PAIN WOKE Talia long before the sun had risen. She wanted to call for a nurse, but didn't want any more of the narcotics that had kept her in a stupor since the surgery. Had it been two days now? Her mind was so cloudy she couldn't be sure.

The room she was in was different, smaller, and two walls were windows with the shades drawn. The door was open and she could hear beeping and hushed voices.

She looked at her bedside table for her cell phone. She needed to call Kelly, but she had no idea where her phone was. A pink water pitcher and a box of tissues were the only items on the table. The hospital phone was gone too. She needed to hear Kelly's voice and know that everything would be okay. Talia had to make sure Kelly wouldn't leave her now that she was—was what? Crippled? Maimed? How could she describe it? This was a hell of a way to lose weight. That thought made her laugh bitterly through the tears that suddenly misted her eyes.

She grabbed the tissues and threw the box across the room. The action did nothing to satisfy her and made her belly hurt like hell. She was still tender from her internal surgeries, and now had to contend with losing a leg.

And maybe losing Kelly, too.

Tears streamed down her cheeks and she angrily wiped them away, but that didn't stop them from coming. She couldn't stop looking at how the blanket was flat where her leg should be.

"How can my leg be gone?" she said to the empty room. "I can feel it. I know it's there, but when I look for it—"

"Talia?" The soft-spoken voice startled her and Talia looked to the doorway. Dr. Lin, a slim Asian woman with light footsteps, came into the room. She had her hands in the pockets of her white lab coat and a smile that was way too cheery for the early hour.

"Dr. Lin, why can I still feel my leg?" Talia pointed needlessly to the missing appendage. "And it hurts. What's going on? And why am I in a new room?"

"You're in ICU until tomorrow. We need to keep an eye on you. It's standard procedure after the surgery you've had." She picked up the chart from the foot of the bed, and paged through it. "As for the pain, some amputees report feeling what is termed phantom pains. These should lessen over time."

"There's nothing phantom here. The pain is real."

"Yes, I realize that. You see, the brain thinks it's still receiving information, despite the fact that the leg is gone. Trust me when I tell you that this will get better. It may never go away completely, though. I can prescribe you some pain pills if you'd like."

"No. I don't want more drugs. Can you explain why? Why did you have to amputate?"

Dr. Lin replaced the chart and moved to stand next to the rail on the hospital bed. "The infection couldn't be stopped. We tried several antibiotics, and the last surgery was supposed to help drain the infection. Nothing was working. The only way to stop it was to amputate your leg. Otherwise the infection could have spread to your bloodstream and that could be fatal."

"Is the infection gone now?"

"We won't know for a while. I expect it to clear up quickly now. We'll test your blood, keep you on the antibiotics, but I feel we removed enough of the bad tissue." Dr. Lin patted her on the arm in a rare display of good bedside manner. "Talia, you're going to be fine. You'll be moved to a regular room in the morning, and in a few more days, you'll be out of here and on your way to Drake Hospital where you can start your rehab and get a temporary prosthesis. It won't be long before you'll be up and walking like this never happened."

"I wish I felt your optimism, Doctor."

"You will. Just give yourself some time." Dr. Lin stood. "I have to prep for surgery. Don't hesitate to have the nurses call me if needed."

"Can you call someone for me?"

"Who?"

"My friend Kelly McCoy. I need Kelly to be here."

"Is she a relative?"

"Close enough." Talia looked at the doctor. "Please. I need her here. Will you make sure she's on the list of visitors allowed in?"

"Sure, and I'll have the nurse get you a phone. Okay?"

"Thanks."

JACOB'S VOICE WAS soft. "I'm here, honey." He combed Talia's hair with his fingers. "You okay?"

"Groggy still. Is Kelly here?"

"She stepped out to use the restroom." Jacob said. "The Queen Mother left before we got here, thank God."

"How long have I been asleep?"

"You called me at about seven-thirty this morning and it's after one now."

"Wow. Glad I slept through Mother's visit. I don't think I can handle her right now."

"She told the nurses she'd be back this evening."

"Can I come in?" Kelly called from the doorway.

Talia looked past Jacob and burst into tears. Kelly was at her side in an instant, pulling Talia into a gentle embrace. "Oh, baby, it's okay. I'm here."

Talia couldn't speak. She sobbed into Kelly's shoulder until she was sure she had no tears left. Jacob kept a steady supply of tissues coming her way.

After a while, Kelly sat on the bed beside her and used a tissue to dry Talia's face. "Better?"

"Yeah," Talia squeaked. "Jacob, could I have some water?"

"Of course," he said and poured some into a little Styrofoam cup.

Talia sipped the cool liquid and tried to compose herself. She hadn't expected to be so emotional when she saw Kelly. But she'd needed her so badly. And she was here. Kelly hadn't disappeared for good after all.

"I'm sorry I couldn't be here when you had the surgery," Kelly said.

"It's okay," Talia lied, and by the expression on Kelly's face, she knew it. Her eyes filled with tears again. "So it wasn't okay, but you're here now. That's all that matters."

"I promised you I'd be here, baby." Kelly held Talia's hands in hers. "You really need to understand that I care about you, Talia Stoddard. Seriously."

"It's hard."

Kelly brought Talia's hands to her lips and planted a kiss across her knuckles. "I'm not leaving. You've got a long road ahead, and I plan to be right by your side. Got it?"

"I got it." Talia felt like crying again, and Kelly wrapped her up in another embrace that soothed her enough that she didn't burst into tears. "What did I ever do to deserve you?"

"Got hit by a ton of bricks?" Kelly laughed, and the sound brought a smile to Talia's face. She drew back enough to look into Kelly's eyes and saw tears forming there. She looked at Kelly's lips, so warm and inviting. She fought hard for the courage to kiss her and couldn't quite marshal the strength.

It was a good thing Talia didn't have to. Kelly leaned closer and kissed her on the mouth, a light kiss, but a lingering one that Talia felt long after Kelly pulled away.

"Um, did you two forget I'm here or what?" Jacob said. He gently pushed Kelly out of his way and gave Talia a hug. "Look, I'll let you two be alone. I can see you're in good hands."

Talia said, "I'm sorry, Jacob."

"Don't be." He kissed her cheek. To Kelly he said, "You take care of her and call me if anything changes."

"Done." Kelly sat on the edge of Talia's bed and watched Jacob leave. "I feel bad for ignoring him."

"You have nothing to worry about. He wasn't being serious. Except for the part where he said to call. That was serious."

"Hmm." Kelly kissed Talia again, her lips warm and soothing. "Just didn't want you to forget how serious I am."

"I don't think I can."

"Young lady," the familiar voice of Talia's mother announced from the doorway, "you are not family and need to leave."

Talia wanted to argue, but Kelly put her fingers to her lips. "Shh. It's not worth it. Just rest and try to get through this time with your mother, and I promise I'll come back in a few hours." With a lingering look, Kelly quietly left.

"The nerve of that woman." Colette's face twisted in anger. "I should report her."

"Report her? What are you talking about?"

"She's not family."

Yes she is, Talia thought. Aloud she said, "She's my girlfriend and I put her and Jacob on the visitor's list." Did she just say girlfriend? The word was so natural and felt so good to say.

"Oh, no, you're not going to start this nonsense again."

"I don't want to argue with you. I'd rather we forget it and let me rest."

Colette settled into a chair obviously discomfited by the situation with Kelly. Talia had to admit that she enjoyed seeing her mother out of her element. Usually Colette Stoddard was so bossy, so in charge, so entirely in control...and right now, she couldn't get her controlling fingers around the situation.

After a few moments, Talia settled down and felt sleepy again. Colette's voice cut through the drowsiness, and Talia opened her eyes.

"How are you feeling? Has the doctor been in to see you?"

"She was here this morning. My leg still hurts and my head is still a little woozy from the drugs."

"Your leg hurts? I thought it was okay. Did the doctor examine it?"

"No, Mother, you don't understand. The leg they took—I can still feel it."

"That's not possible. How can you feel something that isn't there?"

"The doctor said it was phantom pains. My brain is telling me it's there and it hurts, even though it's gone." Talia leaned back in her bed. The whole conversation was giving her a headache.

"Must be all in your head then. You just get some rest. I'm sure everything will be fine when you wake up." Colette took a book from her oversized purse. "I'll be here when you wake up, in case you need anything."

That didn't bode well for Kelly sneaking back in. Talia wanted to comment, to encourage her mom to go, but sleep beckoned and seemed like a much better place to be.

Chapter
Sixteen

SMOKE AND FLAMES engulfed a four-story apartment complex. Most of the top floor was gone, the roof having collapsed earlier. Kelly and Scott were part of the group of firefighters sent to control the blaze on the third floor.

They had done a sweep of all the rooms to ensure no one remained inside. The heat was intense. Kelly was on her knees, one arm holding the hoseline, the other holding an axe as she and Scott crawled through the blackened hallway.

Sweat formed on her forehead despite the protective mask she was wearing. For the last few minutes, she'd been watching the gauge inside the mask that gave her the pressure on her air bottle. She still had another five minutes of breathing air left. Knowing her partner as well as she did, that meant Scott had about two minutes left.

She tapped him on the shoulder and pointed behind them toward the window they'd come in through. She wanted to work their way back so they could get out before he used up his air.

Scott nodded his head and they turned to retrace their steps. They had to stop twice to douse flames on their way to their exit. When they were at the window, Kelly grabbed the nozzle from Scott and yelled, "Out!"

Scott hesitated, but she shoved him toward the window. He had less air than she did and she wanted him out first. She aimed the water at flames roaring around the entrance to the room, but had a feeling it was too little too late.

Scott lifted his legs one at a time over the windowsill and descended the ladder.

Kelly continued to put water on the fire but it wouldn't stop spreading along the walls of the hallway. Despite her efforts the heat was rising. She tossed the nozzle down and leaned out the window to grab the end of the ladder. Before she could get over the window sill and descend, she heard a roar behind her and felt a burst of hot air so strong it pushed her out the window.

She was flung around like a ragdoll, sure she was going to fall sixty feet to her death. She didn't know how, but her utility belt ended up tangled in the top end of the ladder. She hung there for a few terrifying seconds, unable to move.

A flurry of movement below. Shouts. She couldn't understand

their directions, so she stayed still, gripping ladder rungs and feeling entirely helpless as the intense heat from the fire scorched her. How long would the air bottle last? Any minute now, she'd be sucking in the belching smoke. She tried to disentangle herself, with no luck.

The vibration of heavy footfalls smashed their way up the ladder. Strong hands helped to right her, to keep her steady so she could unhook her belt. Kelly didn't waste a moment getting herself together. She descended, hampered only by Scott's slightly slower progress.

Several of the guys from her station slapped her on the back when she got down. Scott helped her out of her air pack and though she announced she was okay, Jimmy ordered her to the rehab area to take a break. It was one of the rare times that Kelly didn't argue about him pulling her from a working fire.

Scott left her and went to refill their air bottles. Kelly let her fellow paramedics give her a once-over, then stretched out to rest, lying on her back with her hands behind her head, on the grass next to the ambulance. She needed a few minutes to remove the image of the blast catapulting her out the window, fire shooting behind her and feeling the heat through her thick protective clothing. She could still physically feel that moment when she was airborne, out of control, and unable to do a damn thing about it. What would have happened if she hadn't gotten hung up? She shivered.

When she felt a little more put together, she'd rejoin her unit to work on overhaul, clearing away debris and checking to make sure there were no hotspots in the walls or anywhere in the building. It was going to be a long day. The sun was high in the sky so she figured it must be around noon. The heat of the fire was second only to the heat of a humid June day. She was glad for the little shade in the ambulance shadow.

Heavy footsteps approached, and she figured it was Scott or Jimmy coming to check on her. She opened one eye to see Jason Burke standing a couple of feet away. "What's the matter? Little girly can't handle the job?"

"Go to hell, Burke. I was ordered here."

"Like I said. Should never have fucking let women on the job."

"You need something?" Kelly asked. She leaned on her elbow and looked up at the big dunce. "I mean, you're here for a reason, right?"

"I got ordered here 'cause I used two bottles of air."

"Two bottles?" Kelly got to her feet and feigned surprise. "If you were halfway fit, you shouldn't be sucking down that much air. I mean, I was in there longer than you and I never used my whole bottle. Even old man Sanderson didn't use more than one. What's up, Burke? Too out of shape?"

"Dyke, you're asking for an ass-kicking."

"From the guy sucking air like it was beer? Doubt it." She dusted off the front of her pants. "Besides, you probably couldn't get your leg up high enough to kick my ass."

Burke grabbed a piece of Kelly's shirt, lifted her off her feet, and slammed her against the side of the ambulance, pinning her there. "You fucking dyke. You shut your fucking mouth before I make sure you never talk again."

He knocked the breath out of her, and she couldn't respond. She had both of her hands on his meaty fist, trying to pry herself loose. Finally, she choked out, "Fuck you" and kicked him in the groin. It wasn't hard enough to bring him to his knees, but got him to let her go. "You want a fight?" she said, catching her breath. "Then you've got one."

She clipped his chin with a right hook. Her hand hurt, but that didn't stop her from swinging again. She missed and went for a third try, but someone grabbed her from behind.

"Hold on there killer," Scott said. He pulled her away from Burke.

"He started it and I'm going to finish."

"What the hell's going on?" Jimmy bellowed, standing between the two combatants.

Burke said, "That fucking dyke kicked me in the nuts."

"After you slammed me against the ambulance, you stupid prick." Kelly shoved away from Scott. "L-T I want to charge that stupid bastard with assault."

"Assault?" Burke shouted. "You're the one—"

Jimmy held up his hand to quiet them. "Both of you can give me a statement when we get back to the station. We'll clear this up then. Meantime, Burke you get your rehab done. McCoy, you get your ass over to the engine and pack up. I need you and Sanderson on overhaul."

"I'll get our air packs," Scott said and he and Jimmy stalked away.

Kelly turned to go, but froze when she heard Burke's voice, quiet and deadly. "Best keep a look out, dyke. This ain't finished."

"Yes it is," Jimmy said. He'd come back and told Burke to leave. When Burke was gone, Jimmy turned to Kelly. "What the hell is wrong with you?"

"He was being a dick so I gave it back to him. You should've let me kick his ass."

"No. I should be writing you up, but I'm not going to. You're getting a verbal warning because you damn near got hurt. If you're not ready to go back in, I'll get someone else."

"No, I'm good. I guess he just pushed my buttons, L-T. I'll

apologize to him if you want me to."

"I'll put that in writing," Jimmy said. "Now get your ass in there for overhaul."

"Copy that."

Chapter
Seventeen

TALIA READ THE note for the tenth time that morning. Reading it made her sympathize with the archaeologists who studied the hieroglyphics of ancient Egypt. But she got the gist of it. Kelly had stopped by, she'd been asleep, and it had been important for her to let Talia know she'd been there.

It sucked that she was still so damn sleepy all the time, and sucked even more that she'd missed a visit with Kelly. But the short note meant more to her than Talia thought possible. She had no idea if a relationship with Kelly would work, but she knew she wanted one.

"Miss Stoddard?"

Her mother's lawyer walked into her room. Talia pointed at the door. "Leave. I don't have anything to say to you, Mr. Clark."

Delmar Clark continued walking toward her bed and placed a briefcase on the empty rolling table. "This will only take a minute."

"I don't think you heard me. Get out of here." Talia's voice got louder and her hand hovered close to the nurse's call button.

"I heard you," he said, shuffling through some papers. "Ah, here it is." He put the paper in front of her and held out a pen. "I need you to sign this and I'm out of here."

"I'm not signing anything."

"Look, this won't take more than a few seconds and it will be worth millions to you."

Talia narrowed her gaze at the man with beady eyes and a face that reminded her of a ferret. "No. I don't want your lawsuit or your money. Now get out before I call the nurse."

Clark was fast and had the call button out of her hand in a flash. "No. Sign the paper. Please."

"You're an ambulance-chasing bastard." She tore the paper in half. "Bite me."

"Look, I'm trying to do you a favor. I can get you a seven figure settlement without ever stepping into court."

"I don't care. I'm not suing the family of that poor man."

"That poor man nearly killed you. He crippled you for life." He touched the empty space on the bed where her leg should have been. "It's his fault you don't have a leg."

Talia stared at his hand, feeling anger welling inside her. But it wasn't the anger she suspected Delmar Clark wanted her to have.

She wasn't angry with the dead man's family or with Mr. Colwell. She was angry at this lawyer for conning her mother into the lawsuit to start with. "I'm not signing anything. My lawyer's name is Jacob Meier, and if anything is done in court or otherwise, it'll be by him."

Clark stepped back from her bed at the mention of Jacob. "Really? He doesn't have the—"

"He has more than you'll have in your whole lifetime, Mr. Clark." Talia finished the sentence for him, not wanting to hear what he had to say. "So get out of my room before I call security."

Clark gathered his things and moved to the door. "You'll regret this. I could have made you a millionaire."

"Money isn't everything, Mr. Clark. And I don't regret anything other than my mother's vulnerability."

Clark looked like he had something else to say, but Talia continued. "I don't expect to hear from you or see you again. If I do, I'll have my lawyer file a restraining order. Is that clear?"

He didn't respond and left the room.

Talia reached for her cell phone and called Jacob. His assistant put her through immediately.

"Hi, sweetie!" His voice was cheery and high pitched.

"Hi, Jacob. Can you talk?"

"Hang on." She heard muffled speech in the background. A door slammed shut and Jacob came back to the phone. "Men. Can't live with 'em, can't kill 'em."

"Boy troubles again?"

"Oh, honey, it's more complicated than you need to know. So, what's up?"

"Delmar Clark."

"Ick. That name gives me a rash." She heard Jacob's chair creaking as he leaned back in it. "Did he contact you again? I called his office and told him to stay away."

"He was here." She recounted how the stubborn lawyer had treated her.

"I'll take care of him, sweetie. I already have the restraining order filled out and ready for your signature. I'll bring it with me at lunch and get it to the judge today. You won't hear from that cockroach again."

"Have I said I love you today?"

"No, but please do. I need to feel the love."

"I love you, Jacob. Very much. Thanks for taking care of this for me."

"No problem. It's nice to be able to squash the insect. It's the fun part of my job."

"And why I love you. See? I said it three times."

"Ah, but you really love me for my mind and my incredible body."

"You have an incredible body?" Talia giggled harder when Jacob refused to answer her. "Oh, honey, don't be mad."

"I could never be mad at you. I better go fix things."

Talia's eyes grew wide when she realized Kelly was in the room. "Got to go, Jacob. Bye." She disconnected the call and dropped her cell phone into her lap. "Hi there. I was, um, talking to Jacob."

"You're cute when you blush."

"I do not blush." She gave her a mock look of ferocity.

"Oh, yeah, you do. You get this adorable sheepish look and — see! You're doing it again."

Talia ducked a little so Kelly couldn't see her, but she didn't miss the coffee container and brown paper bag Kelly set on the bed table. "Breakfast."

"Bless you!"

"I'm starved, but I didn't realize you'd be that hungry, too." She pulled out a blueberry bagel and cream cheese and handed it to Talia, then picked up her own cinnamon one and bit into it. Chewing, she said, "Don't they feed you here?"

"Have you ever tasted hospital food?"

"Once, when I was ten and had my tonsils removed. I got all the ice cream I wanted and didn't complain once."

"Ha ha. I'd kill for some ice cream."

Kelly said, "I'll make sure I bring some next time. I'd tell you to ask your nurse to get you some, but you'll probably only get those tiny little containers of crappy ice with freezer burn."

"You sound like an expert."

"Paramedics know where anything that resembles food can be found."

Talia sipped her coffee and made yummy sounds when she was done. "You really are my hero, bringing me real coffee."

"I just love catering to a lady." Kelly kissed her.

"I wasn't sure you'd come this morning."

"Of course I'm here. I told you I'd stop by after my shift was over."

"I know. It's just that — you keep on coming back. Why me? What's so special about me?"

Kelly was at a loss for words. Talia was so important to her, but how could she make her understand that? How could she explain that she was falling in love with her? "I've never met anyone like you. I mean, I feel like I've known you forever. You're so easy for me to talk to."

"No one's ever said that to me before."

"It's true. I want you to know everything about me."

"I'd like that."

"There's something I haven't told anyone I'm close to, except my mom knows, of course, and Scott."

"What's that?"

"You know I'm from New York, and I told you I got rid of the accent because I don't like people asking about 9-11, right? I don't want the questions because I was there. I was in the city that day, and I worked the pile until my hands and feet were bleeding."

"The pile?" Talia asked.

"Ground Zero." Kelly paused to compose her words. She wanted to—needed to—tell Talia about this life-changing event. The news had reported the facts and some stories from those that lost friends and loved ones, but that never felt like it was enough. "There were some stress counselors there, walking around the pile talking to us and helping us work. I'll never forget it..."

Kelly stopped for a second to wipe the sweat from her brow, then sat in the chair next to Talia's bed.

"You okay?" Talia asked.

Kelly said, "Yeah, just give me a minute here."

It was all too easy to transport herself back to the horrors of that time. Usually Kelly did all she could to avoid thinking about it. Today the memories were close, almost visceral. She remembered how the heat coming from beneath the rocks was incredible. She was on her second pair of boots in two days and wondering how long these would last. She looked around her at the rest of the rescuers on the bucket line. Most were FDNY, but the woman beside her wore a white construction helmet with "OHIO" on the front.

Kelly was so tired that all she really wanted to do was sleep. But that wasn't an option. She had to keep going. Had to keep working. If no one was left alive, the least she could do was continue to help remove the rubble so that maybe they would find the remains of some of her brothers.

The woman beside her worked quietly as Kelly handed her bucket after bucket laden with debris. "Where you from in Ohio?"

The woman looked up at her. "Dayton. North of Cincinnati."

"You a firefighter?"

"Yep." She held out her hand. "Lee-Jean."

"Kelly." They shook in greeting. "How long you been here?"

"Just a few days. You?"

"Since Day One." Kelly gazed out over the rubble. Not one of the FDNY men were familiar, and she was slowly getting used to that. It was like being a stranger in your own home, but at the same time, she knew these strangers were her brother and sister firefighters, and cops and medics, and that meant more than anything. "Most of my station is somewhere under this pile."

"Have you found any of them?"

"Two. Dead." Kelly wasn't sure why she shared this with a complete stranger, but it didn't matter. She needed to share. "Both were guys I've known most of my life. My dad was an engineer at the same house I work at."

"Family business. Seems like a trend in this city."

"Pretty much."

"Does your dad still work there?"

"No. He died in the line a few years ago."

"Sorry to hear that."

"I'm thankful. I wouldn't want him to have to deal with this."

"How are you dealing with it?" Lee-Jean asked.

Kelly hesitated. She hadn't thought about it much. Though none of the firefighters from her station house had been found alive, she had worked the first few days with a fervent hope of finding someone.

Now, two weeks later, she knew it wasn't going to happen, but she'd been so focused on the physical task, she didn't know how to answer Lee-Jean. "I don't think I am." Kelly dropped the bucket she held and made her way down the mountain of rubble. She heard someone behind her, but couldn't bring herself to look back. She had managed to work without so much as a thought about herself or her own feelings. Now, in a strange sense of shock, she felt them all coming to the surface.

She sat on the remains of a bench, put her head into her hands and wept.

Some time later, someone sat beside her and placed a towel in her hands. She used it to wipe her face, and then leaned back on the bench.

Lee-Jean handed her a bottle of water. Kelly took it without speaking and drank to soothe a thirst she hadn't realized was there.

"I brought you a sandwich, too." Lee-Jean held out a plastic dish of food. "You need to eat."

"Thanks." Kelly accepted it and took her time chewing. She washed the turkey sandwich down with the rest of her water and smiled when Lee-Jean handed her another bottle. "Always prepared?"

"Yep." Lee-Jean said.

"I really didn't expect to get all emotional like that."

"You had to let it out sometime."

"Not now. Not when there's so much work to be done."

"Kelly, there are hundreds of workers here. And thousands more waiting to help. It's okay if you need to take a break and compose yourself. You've suffered a great loss, and it's a normal, human reaction to feel like this."

"I don't think I can sit here and rest." Kelly looked at the pile of rubble and all the workers still diligently trying to clear it. "I've gotta help find them."

"I know you feel that way, but you can't do it without rest. If you don't take care of yourself, you won't be any good to anyone." Lee-Jean placed a hand on her shoulder. "You still have family?"

"Yeah. My mom is at home. I try to call her when I can, but I get so busy."

"Just make sure you're taking care of yourself for her. She needs you."

"I know." Kelly closed her eyes. "Thanks, Lee-Jean."

"Anytime." She removed a pin from her pocket and attached it to Kelly's t-shirt. Kelly looked down to see a tiny figure in white, a golden halo over her head and her hands outstretched in prayer. "A guardian angel to watch over you."

"You really think I have one?"

Lee-Jean looked at the pile, then back at Kelly "We've got hundreds of them looking over us right now." She patted her on the shoulder and stood. "Get some rest?"

"I'll try. Thanks." Kelly watched as Lee-Jean returned to the pile. The back of her white helmet had the letters CISM written on it. Critical Incident Stress Management. Kelly realized now that Lee-Jean was a peer counselor and not just another worker on the pile.

She couldn't remember how she'd gotten through the rest of those endless hours of searching. They never found five of her friends and it was like someone had turned off a switch in her heart. She couldn't feel. She couldn't think. How could she explain how alone and inadequate she'd felt?

But Talia was there and listening to every word she said. She needed someone to know and telling Talia felt right. She stumbled through a description of what happened and how she'd felt, and when she was done, all she saw was concern and acceptance on Talia's face.

"That's amazing," Talia said as she wiped tears from her cheeks. "It must have been so hard for you."

"It was. And it will be for a long time, but the point is that I managed to get counseling. Not just that day, but ever since it happened." Kelly sighed. "At first I thought it would make me weak...not being able to handle the job. But I realized after a while that I was a normal person dealing with an abnormal situation. It wasn't any surprise my defense mechanisms were overloaded, you know?"

"I think it was that way for the whole country, but so much worse for you all who were actually there."

"Maybe. But it's not so hard today. And it won't be as hard

tomorrow. Do you see what I'm getting at?"

"That it's taken you years to deal with 9-11?"

"No." Kelly said. "That I've learned to understand my feelings. I wanted to share this with you because it's part of who I am. I grew up around the fire service, and I live and breathe it today. Maybe it's even more important to me now than it was when I first started ten years ago.

"Anyway, Ma and I did our best to get back to our lives after it was all over. But it was never really over.

"There were funerals to go to. It was hard for all of us, but Ma couldn't stand seeing me put on that dress uniform every few days.

"Ever since my dad's funeral, Ma has been weird about me continuing in the fire service. We moved out here because it's a slower pace, a smaller department, and I'm on the medic unit more than the engine. Ma likes that part." Kelly grinned. "But she's always behind me. No matter what."

"I'm glad you told me." Talia kissed her softly.

Kelly rested her head against Talia's shoulder and sighed. "Me, too. Feels like I've got this weight lifted off my shoulders."

"Good." Talia ran her fingers through Kelly's hair. "Thanks for sharing it with me."

Tears filled Kelly's eyes and a knot that had formed long ago in her stomach seemed to ease. She couldn't reply because, for the first time in years, she felt safe.

Chapter
Eighteen

TALIA WASN'T SURE what a rehabilitation center would look like, but Drake Hospital didn't seem much different than the hospital she'd just left. The ambulance crew was nice to her on the way there, but she wished all the while that Kelly were there with her.

The double room she was assigned had an empty bed, and she wondered briefly if she would have a roommate. Her mother would probably insist that she have a private room. Talia didn't look forward to that fight.

After the ambulance crew got her situated in the new bed, her nurse greeted her. He was tall and muscular with a movie-star smile and the tan to go with it. Jacob was going to be jealous.

"Hi there. I'm Brad, your nurse for today. How was the ride over?"

"Thankfully short." Talia said. She tried get comfortable in the new bed, but nothing eased the pain in her leg.

"Sore?"

"Yeah. I've been having sharp pains in my leg all morning. The moving around hasn't helped much."

"Dr. Lin prescribed some Demerol for you." Brad made a few notes on her chart. "You need anything else?"

"I'd love some water, please."

"Sure. Be right back." Brad left, and Talia noticed his little swagger when he walked. Yes, Jacob was going to enjoy visiting.

Her few belongings were in a bag on the bedside table. She dug to the bottom for her cell phone, surprised when it started ringing. She pressed the answer key the second she had it in her hand. "Hello?"

"Hey baby," Kelly said. "How do you like the new place? Are you settled in?"

"Just got here." Talia looked around at the bare walls and the empty corkboard on the wall opposite her bed. "It's boring, tidy, and very, very white. Why don't you come over and add some color to it."

"Hey, are you making fun of my hair?"

"I wouldn't dream of it. Though you have to admit that it does brighten up a room."

"Hmm. I'm going to have to make you pay for that remark." Her voice was low and suggestive.

"I look forward to it." Talia couldn't believe they were flirting over the phone. Nobody she'd ever dated had been so carefree about such things. For all she knew, Kelly could be at the firehouse or in a store. "Are you coming over today?"

"I'm just stepping foot inside the front door of the hospital. What's your room number?"

"Sure you don't want to hunt me down?" Talia laughed, then said, "112" and closed the cell phone. She waited for Kelly, grinning happily when she saw her walk through her door. "Smart ass."

"Uh huh." Kelly crossed the room quickly and kissed her on the lips. Her hand lingered on the side of Talia's face.

Talia shivered with pleasure, delighted that Kelly felt comfortable enough to kiss her and touch her.

"I wanted to make sure you were settled in. I'm kind of surprised your mother didn't beat me to it though."

"She's gone to get lunch and said she'd come see me afterwards." Talia patted the bed. "Have a seat?"

"Love to." Kelly sat on the side of the bed near Talia's good leg. "You feeling okay? You look a bit pale."

"It hurts. A lot."

"Did you ask for some pain meds?"

"Got the cure right here," Brad announced as he entered the room. He had a syringe in one hand and a pitcher of ice water in the other. "Hey, Kelly."

"Hi, Brad." She patted Talia's arm. "At least now I know you'll be in good hands."

"You know each other?"

Kelly said, "We went to paramedic class together."

"Yeah, small world in the medical field." Brad injected the medication into Talia's IV. "Won't be long before this takes effect and you'll probably feel sleepy."

"I'm getting used to that," Talia said. "But thanks."

"Okay. Enjoy your visit." Brad waved to them on his way out.

"He's a sweetheart." Kelly adjusted the blanket around Talia. "He'll take good care of you."

"Better care than you have?" Talia placed her hand over Kelly's. "Thanks for being here."

"Where else would I be?" Kelly's mouth covered Talia's in a kiss so sweet Talia felt like crying.

Her brain screamed that this was a dream, something she couldn't expect or hope for, but Kelly's hands, the touch of her lips, the sound of her voice, it was all very real. Talia hoped she wouldn't do something to screw it all up.

When they came up for air, Kelly said, "I can't stay long today."

"Can you come by tomorrow?"

"Sorry, gotta work. But I did bring you this." Kelly pulled a small calendar from her back pocket. "It's what we call a shift calendar. I'm on shift B, so any day you see a 'B' you know that I'm working. Unless it's Friday. I always have Friday off."

"That sounds confusing." Talia flipped through the pages and found where Kelly had marked her days off.

"I tried to make it easy for you." She kissed Talia again. "I should go before your mother arrives. Remember you can call me, even if I'm working. I might be on a job, but leave a message and I'll call back as soon as I can."

"You're so sweet." Talia cupped the side of Kelly's face, wishing she didn't have to leave. "Can't wait to see you again."

"Me either." Kelly turned her head and kissed Talia's palm, then pressed her lips to Talia's one last time before leaving the room.

Talia could still feel Kelly's touch as she fell asleep.

IT FELT LIKE minutes, rather than hours later when Talia woke up to find her mother seated beside the bed. She blinked a few times to let her vision focus and what she saw surprised her.

Colette Stoddard wore a black dress, high heel shoes, and a pearl necklace that Talia had only ever seen her wear to funerals and weddings.

"Hi Mother. Was your lunch good?"

"It was edible. This town lacks in good restaurants." Colette shifted uncomfortably in the chair. "I certainly hope they don't plan to put another person in here with you. You need your rest and privacy."

"If they do, I'm sure I'll be okay. It's not a big deal."

Colette brushed invisible lint from her dress. "It is to me. You need to be left alone after all you've been through."

Had she just heard a hitch in her mother's voice? "Can I ask why you're so dressed up? Did you meet someone for lunch?"

Colette wouldn't meet Talia's gaze. "Your father."

Talia felt her stomach clench. "I'm afraid to ask."

"I wanted him to talk some sense into you over this lawsuit." Colette straightened.

"He won't. Daddy agrees with me on the lawsuit. No one could have known that man would drive his truck into the building. I survived. That's why Kelly is so special—"

"Please don't speak of her."

"You have to learn to accept who I am. And Kelly is becoming a big part of my life."

"Are you involved with her?"

"Yes," Talia surprised herself with the quick answer. "It's a little awkward with me in here, but the moment I'm able to she's promised to take me out. She cares about me and she's been there for me in a way no other woman ever has."

"Talia. You've only known her a couple of weeks. How could you possibly be so close?"

"You have no idea what we've shared together. We were in that debris pile for nearly two hours. It felt more like days. She risked her life to take care of me. Since then, she hasn't let me down. She told me about her experiences on 9-11, and I've shared a lot about my life too. There's just something special about her. Please try to understand."

"She feels sorry for you." Colette stood. After brushing the wrinkles from her dress, she adjusted the blanket. "Megan will be here tomorrow."

"Why? I told her to leave me alone."

"She's determined to make you give her another chance."

"Megan or you?" Talia watched her mother closely and knew the answer by the clenching of her jaw muscles. "I thought so. Mother, you can tell Megan she's wasting her time. I'm happy with Kelly."

"We'll see." Colette picked up her purse and started out of the room. "I'll bring Megan to see you after I get her settled at the hotel."

Chapter
Nineteen

KELLY'S SHIFT STARTED off bad when she found out she had ambulance duty. Again. It would make her fourth straight shift as a paramedic and she itched to get back on the engine. She didn't mind the medical part of the job, but fire fighting was in her blood. At the age of four, she'd gone on her first ride on a truck and never looked back.

"This sucks." She slammed the cabinet drawer shut after completing a check of its contents. The checklist completed, she decided to get a cup of coffee. She stepped onto the bumper and the alert tones sounded. "Fuck."

The dispatcher announced a woman down at an apartment building a few blocks from the fire station. "Possible non-breather," she reported.

"Double fuck," Kelly said and jumped down, then closed the back doors of the vehicle. Scott ran from the driver's side as she got in the passenger seat.

"8:25. I think that's a record. Last shift our first run came at 8:03."

"Did you do something to piss Jimmy off?"

"Why?" Scott turned on the lights and sirens and pulled out on to the street.

"It's our fourth shift on the box. I'm getting to think he's mad at us."

Scott shrugged. "Just got lucky."

"Lucky? If this is luck, I don't want luck anymore. And I sure don't want a damn code."

"Grouchy much? Wait. Did you get your coffee yet?"

"No."

"That explains everything."

"Bite me," Kelly took a deep breath as they pulled up to the building. She got out and headed in without another word to her partner.

"What happened?" Kelly asked as she entered the small apartment.

"I don't know," the elderly man that greeted her hobbled toward a hallway. "She's in the bedroom. I woke up and she wasn't breathing."

Kelly eased past him and started toward the room. Scott finally caught up to her and started asking the man for information. "When did you last see her?"

"When we went to bed last night."

Scott asked him to stay in the hallway as they entered the bedroom.

The elderly woman lay on her back on the left side of the bed. Kelly set her equipment on the floor and checked to see if the woman was breathing. Her skin was cold and her face was nearly purple with small white blotches on her cheeks and neck. Kelly felt for a pulse and found none. With one look, she told Scott that the woman was dead.

The level of rigor mortis suggested she had died hours ago. "Is her husband still out there?"

Scott nodded. "Yeah. I'll go tell him and disregard the engine crew." He gathered up his gear and left.

Kelly stood in the room for a few seconds to look around. Nothing appeared out of order. She was about to leave when she saw the picture. An old photo, maybe from the 1940's, hung beside the door frame, next to the switch plate for the light. A simple wood frame held the photo, but it was elegant. The young man she imagined was the same man who had met them at the door. He was wearing an army uniform and grinning proudly.

The photo was black and white. His eyes held a hint of mischief in them and the crinkle in his nose made her smile back. He had stripes on his sleeves indicating the rank of sergeant. Just below his chin were some words. Though she knew the message was private, Kelly felt compelled to read it anyway.

"To my dearest Ella, I fell in love with you the moment I first saw you at the Spring Social. You are my heart, my soulmate and I wouldn't be worth a nickel without you. I'll love you always darling, Frank."

Kelly stepped back from the photo and wiped at the sudden tears in her eyes. His soulmate. She glanced back at the peaceful face of the woman on the bed. "She must have been pretty when she was young."

"Most beautiful woman I've ever seen."

Kelly was startled to find the man, Frank, standing behind her. "I'm sorry for your loss, sir."

"Thank you." His eyes were on his wife as the man slowly made his way to her side. He dropped to his knees beside the bed, took her hand in his and began to weep.

Kelly quickly stepped out of the room and made a hasty retreat to find Scott.

"Cops will be here in about five minutes."

"Good. I'll get the equipment back on the bus." She was out the door before Scott could respond.

EXHAUSTION KEPT HER awake most of the night and the moment Kelly's tour was over, she left the fire house. Hospital visiting hours would start soon and she wanted to see Talia. Needed to see her.

She got into her car, turned the key, but didn't move to put it in gear. The strength just wasn't there to move her hand. Kelly stared out the window until her vision blurred and the tears came.

Frank and Ella were married 62 years. Frank told her this as they were leaving. 62 years of marriage with four children and twelve grandchildren to show for it. Kelly couldn't even imagine knowing any one person for that many years and certainly couldn't imagine being with the same person for that long.

Kelly rested her forehead on the steering wheel between her clenched fists. Did she want to be with one person that long? And if she did, what would happen to her partner when Kelly died?

The fire department didn't recognize domestic partners and it would be a cold day in hell when the Religious Right of Ohio allowed gay marriage to be legalized.

Would Talia be okay without her? Who would care for her?

Kelly sat up and wiped her face clean of the tears. How had Talia gotten into this train of thought?

But Kelly knew the answer to that question. Talia was always in her thoughts. And the more time she spent with her, the more Kelly was growing to love the woman. Or maybe it was simply that Kelly was already in love with her.

An old joke about lesbians and moving vans came to mind and Kelly chuckled. It wasn't so much of a joke as it was a real thought in her mind. She really did want to move in with Talia. She wanted to care for Talia, settle down with her. Grow old with her.

She put the car into gear and headed for Drake Hospital.

TALIA LOOKED SO peaceful as she slept that Kelly didn't want to wake her. She sat in the chair next to the bed and leaned her head back. If she closed her eyes for just a few minutes, she'd feel so much better.

"Are you planning to sleep there?"

Kelly opened one eye to look at Talia. "Maybe."

"Wouldn't you be more comfy in bed?"

"Um, yes." Kelly scooted the chair around so she was facing Talia. "But I don't see anyone here offering to let me join them, so I picked this teeny tiny chair."

"You poor thing." Talia patted the bed beside her. "Care to join me?"

"Thought you'd never ask." Kelly put the rail down. Talia moved over as much as she could. Only a few inches of room remained. Kelly lay on her side, balancing to keep from falling off. "Honey, I think we need a bigger bed."

"Sorry." Talia tried to scoot further toward the opposite edge, but it didn't give Kelly any more room.

"No problem. I'll live."

"You can't possibly be comfortable."

Kelly slipped her arm around Talia's body and snuggled closer to her. "It's really quite cozy. Don't you think?"

"What the hell is going on here?"

Kelly nearly fell off the bed, but managed to right herself and get to her feet. Colette Stoddard did not look happy. "We were just—"

"I know what you were doing. I suggest you leave."

"Mother, Kelly has every right to be here." Talia pressed a button and raised the bed so she was sitting up.

"It's okay, Talia. I should probably go home anyway."

"No. You stay right where you are," Talia said, glaring at her mother.

"If you're doing this to upset me, Talia, it's working."

"I don't care. You can't just come in here and order someone out of my room."

Kelly felt like she was at a tennis match, going back and forth between the two women until she got a headache. They kept sniping at each other and she just wanted to slink out of the room and let them have their privacy. Obviously, Talia and her mother needed to work on some issues.

"Please," she broke in to Colette's tirade. "I need to get some sleep." To Talia she said, "I'll come by tomorrow. I'm off and we can spend some time together. Okay?"

"No." Talia looked like a petulant child. She was so cute Kelly wanted to laugh. "But I guess you're right."

"Good answer," Kelly avoided the steely gaze of Colette and kissed Talia on the cheek. "Call me later."

"Count on it."

Kelly walked around Colette and hurried out of the room. She stepped into the hallway and cringed when she heard them arguing again.

Chapter
Twenty

TALIA AWOKE EARLY the next morning. She hadn't heard
back from Kelly and wondered if she was angry with her. Talia's
mother had been such a bitch to Kelly. Maybe Kelly had enough and
didn't want to come around her anymore. And who could blame her?
What woman wanted at fat chick with a controlling homophobic
mother?

The door to her room opened and a woman dressed in light blue
shirt and slacks came in, breaking Talia from her thoughts. Her
brown hair was in a ponytail, and her smile was almost obnoxious at
such an early hour.

"Good morning, and welcome to Drake Hospital." The cheerful
voice was too much and Talia grumbled a response. "Oh, we're going
to have to work on that attitude. I'm Lucie Granger. Your physical
therapist."

"It's my attitude and I'll keep it, thanks."

"Chuck it aside while I'm here."

"Sure." Talia sat up. "So what time is it?"

Lucie lifted the lid from Talia's breakfast tray, which sat
untouched beside the bed, and wrinkled her nose at it. "Past time to
get up and eat."

"Oh. I thought it was early morning."

"It's quarter past nine."

Talia pushed the button to incline her bed. "Like I said, early
morning."

"How do you like your new room?"

"It looks pretty much like the one at University Hospital."

"Good. That's what we were going for." Lucie laughed. "So,
wanna get started?"

"Already?"

"It's been four days since your surgery. Today we're going to
get some measurements and do a few simple exercises. The sooner
we get going, the sooner you're walking."

"The doctor said I'd be walking in a few months. Is that true?"

"That all depends on you." Lucie lowered the bed rail and
pulled the sheet to the end of the bed. She placed a wheelchair close
and pointed to it. "Optimism, positive thinking, and some hard work
will get you up and walking. Negativity is not allowed. Now get in,
and let's go for a ride."

The physical therapy area looked like a small gym. It reminded Talia of the fitness place Megan had taken her to a couple of times. Her ex had been determined to make her get into shape. Talia only remembered that it felt like pure torture.

She recognized the treadmill and stationary bikes that lined one wall. A couple of complicated looking weight machines were in the center of the room and along the back wall were some contraptions Talia couldn't identify.

Lucie rolled her to a set of parallel bars.

"We're going to get you up on that good leg of yours and see how well you do."

"You and how many helpers?"

"That was almost funny." Lucie put the wheelchair between the bars. "I'll help you stand up. You hold on to the sturdy bars here."

"I don't think I can."

"You can." Lucie stood in front of her and held out her hands. "C'mon. I'm right here."

Talia took hold of Lucie's hands. "I'm scared."

"It's okay. That's to be expected."

"What if I fall?"

"Then I'll get you back up." Lucie smiled kindly. "Up."

"Okay." Talia placed her foot on the floor and let Lucie leverage her to a standing position. When Lucie let go of her hands, Talia grabbed the bars. A sharp, stabbing pain hit her left leg and Talia nearly screamed. "It hurts. Please, I have to sit down."

"But you did it." Lucie helped Talia back into the wheelchair. "And that, dear Talia, was my point. You can do this. You will walk again and I'm going to help you get there."

"I—I can't believe I stood up. Why did it hurt so much? I mean, it hurt in the leg that's not even there."

"We'll work on that. I promise." Lucie unlocked the wheels, pushed the chair to one of the tables behind them and redid the locks. "Now, let's get to work.

TALIA'S FIRST PHYSICAL therapy session lasted close to an hour. She wasn't sure what to make of the perky woman who sounded like a mixture of General Patton and Richard Simmons. Lucie made dozens of measurements of her good leg and her stump and put her through a variety of exercises. Talia felt the strain in her muscles.

When they returned to her room, Lucie gave her some exercises to do between sessions. Talia got through the first set and couldn't raise her left leg anymore. She let it plop onto the bed. "I'm done," she said breathlessly.

"You've only done seven. Three more," Lucie stood beside her, one hand steadying Talia's good leg. "Three more and you can be done."

Talia would have given Lucie a cross look if she'd had the energy. "I'm done. My leg hurts more than it did before we started." She rubbed her thigh for emphasis.

"Okay." Lucie put lotion on her hands. "We'll stop for today. I'm going to give you some light massage, then we'll put some ice on both legs. Sound alright?"

Talia nodded and lay back on bed. Lucie set to working on her leg, her hands warm and firm. The combination of pressure and light strokes didn't hurt at all. She closed her eyes and felt her pain subsiding. "Ahh."

"Feels good?" Lucie asked.

"Very good." She smiled at Lucie, hoping the therapist didn't think she'd been too big of a whiner throughout the session. Talia saw movement across the room and was surprised when Jacob approached.

"Look at you," he said.

"What are you doing here?" Talia asked.

"Bad timing?"

"No, not at all." She introduced Jacob to Lucie. "I just finished my first session of physical therapy."

Jacob eyed Lucie as her hands worked expertly on the muscles of Talia's bad leg. "Hmm. That's my kind of therapy."

Talia ignored his comment. "Please excuse him, Lucie. My friend can be obnoxious sometimes."

"I don't mind." Lucie finished the massage. "I'll get you some ice and you two can visit for a bit."

"Thanks, Lucie."

"Now spill," Jacob said the moment they were alone.

"Spill what?"

He sighed dramatically. "Whatever's bothering you."

"It's nothing."

"Bullshit."

"Jacob—"

"Talia Stoddard."

"Jacob Meier." She mimicked his admonishing tone and they both laughed. "Really, it's just—Mother ran Kelly off yesterday. And not so much as a call or text message since."

"Ever think she might be working?" Talia shrugged. "Or maybe she's actually got a life and hasn't made it up here yet?" Jacob leaned forward and put his hand over hers. "It's hard to believe that even the Queen Mother could run off the woman who stuck by your side when she didn't have to."

"Mother was—"

"A bitch as usual. Trust me, dear friend of mine. Kelly'll be back. I saw the look in her eyes."

"What look?"

He raised one eyebrow. "That look."

Talia thought back to the day before. She didn't recall seeing "that look," as Jacob put it. "You're full of shit, but thanks for trying."

She changed the subject. "What'd you bring me?"

"Nothing."

"Liar."

"Damn. How can you tell?"

Talia giggled. "Because you're the worst liar ever. Hand it over."

He put a small box in her hands. Wrapped with bright pink foil, it didn't weigh more than a few ounces. Talia ripped off the foil and squealed with delight. The tiny electronic device was exactly what she'd been wanting. The iPod had 8 gigabytes of space and a nice set of earbuds so she could listen to her favorite music. The only problem was she didn't know anything about using one.

"You're going to have to show me how this thing works."

"Only if you promise me you'll call Kelly."

"I'm not going to call her. If she wants to talk, she'll call."

"Right. And if everyone said that no one would call anyone." Jacob made a face at her. "I mean it. No using the iPod until you promise me you'll call her."

"What if—"

"Ah ah." He shook his finger at her. "As a matter of fact, call her right now or I'll leave and you'll never figure that thing out." He handed her his phone. "I know how techno stupid you are, so you better dial away, darlin'." He kissed the top of her hand. "You have to learn to trust, honey. She's the real thing."

"I'm scared. What if you're wrong?"

"Won't be the first time."

"What am I supposed to say to her when I call?"

"Tell her you're sorry your mother is a bitch and you want to see her. You'll figure out the rest as you go." Jacob winked at her. "Or you'll be spending all your free time figuring out that iPod."

She stuck her tongue out at him, but accepted her cell phone when he handed it to her. "You're mean."

"No," he leaned back and crossed his arms, "I'm good."

The phone rang several times and Talia was about to hang up when Kelly answered. "Hey, Talia."

"Hi, Kelly. You sound out of breath. Am I calling at a bad time?"

"Nope. Just had to run to get my phone. I was working out."

Talia imagined what Kelly's look like, sweaty, flushed, wearing tight shorts and a sleeveless t-shirt, muscles of her upper arms showing definition as she lifted weights. She heard a snicker and realized Jacob was staring at her and obviously caught on to her train of thought. Talia cleared her throat. "Um, I just wanted to say hi."

"Hi." Kelly laughed. "Your timing sucks, but I'm glad you called. I was thinking about you."

"You were?" Why was that so hard to believe?

"Of course. I've been thinking about coming up there and having a picnic lunch with you. How does that sound?"

"A picnic? With real food?"

Kelly laughed again and the sound warmed Talia's heart. "Of course. I know how hospital food sucks. I'll be over tomorrow and we'll have a nice quiet meal."

"I can't wait."

"Good. I need to get back to my workout before I cool down. Talk to you later?"

"Sure."

"Okay. Bye baby."

"Bye." Talia closed her cell phone and held it against her chest. She tried to ignore the smug look on Jacob's face. "She's bringing me lunch tomorrow."

He buffed his fingers on his chest. "I hate to say I told you so, but I told you so."

"I hate you."

"I know. But that's what makes you so cute. Now, let me show you how to work your iPod."

TALIA OPENED HER eyes and tried to focus on the woman silhouetted against the window. The sun shined brightly, but she knew it was Kelly standing there. "Hey."

"Afternoon, lazy butt. How you feeling?"

"Better. Lucie, the PT Torture Queen, put me through an exhausting workout first thing this morning. Guess I needed a nap." She adjusted the bed so she could sit up. "How long have you been here?"

Kelly shrugged. "Long enough." With a sigh, she moved slowly and leaned on the bed rail. "I've been waiting, actually. I thought you might like to have lunch with me."

"Depends."

"On?"

"Did you bring the food?"

Kelly waggled her eyebrows and pointed to a small cooler by the door. "I would never willingly subject a woman to hospital food. I'm much more suave than that."

"When do we leave?"

Kelly moved a chair out of the way and pulled Talia's wheelchair closer. "Your chariot awaits."

THE COURTYARD OUTSIDE the rehab center's cafeteria was deserted. Talia chalked that up to humid weather, which felt good to her after being cooped up in the air conditioned room for so long.

Kelly rolled her to a black metal bench and angled the chair so they would be facing each other. She pulled a small round table over and spread a red and white checkered cloth over it. She placed two Styrofoam plates, plastic utensils and a big bowl of food onto it. Two bottles of soda completed the arrangement.

"So, would you like me to open your drink for you, madam?"

Talia laughed. "Please. Then let's eat. I'm starved."

The spaghetti salad Kelly had brought was almost gone. Talia sipped on her soda and hid a small belch. "Mmm, you're a good cook." She looked at the remains of lunch and seriously considered seconds, but her mother's voice echoed in her head about gaining weight and she stopped herself.

"Thanks. There's plenty more," Kelly offered, as if she could read Talia's thoughts.

"No, I better not." Her stomach grumbled in protest and both women shared a laugh. "I have to watch my weight."

"What are you watching it do?"

"Ha ha. I'm too fat. Just ask my mother."

Kelly tapped her on the belly. "Your mother is wrong. The extra pounds make you more cuddly. Not fat."

"You're crazy." Talia looked away, hoping to hide her blush.

"No." Kelly cupped Talia's face with one hand. "Look at me."

Talia did and the expression on Kelly's face stole her breath away.

"I'm very serious. There's nothing wrong with you. Not your weight, not your amputated leg—nothing. You're perfect as you are."

"Kel, I—"

"Shh." Kelly touched her fingers to Talia's lips. "No arguing with an Irish woman. You're guaranteed to lose."

Talia couldn't help staring into the most amazing green eyes, never wavering until Kelly removed her fingers. Talia let out a shaky breath, "What did I do to deserve you?"

"You got lucky." Kelly winked at her. "I am, after all, a great catch."

"If you're such a good catch, then why don't I have a box of chocolate to go with this wonderful meal?"

"What makes you so sure you don't?"

"Um, I haven't seen it?"

"And you won't until you've had your meal."

Talia said, "You sound like my mother. No dessert until your food's all gone."

"Yes, but the dessert is well worth the wait."

If you were the dessert... Talia stopped the thought before it could go anywhere, though the tingling in her abdomen let her know that it already had. "I do believe I'm done eating."

"Then dessert it is."

Chapter
Twenty-one

DAYS PASSED, THEN weeks and Talia gradually grew stronger. In a few days, she would be fitted for her first prosthesis and able to go home. All of the exercises she started out unable to do, gradually got easier and she was ready to leave. Her clothes fit looser now and she wondered if she could continue losing weight.

Lucie said she still had several weeks of therapy to go, but all of it would be out-patient now. Talia had just popped one of the sweets Kelly gave her on her last visit into her mouth when her physical therapist, Lucie, came into the room. "Oh, man. You've got rotten timing."

"I hear that a lot." Lucie grabbed a piece of chocolate and parked the wheelchair beside Talia's bed. "Let's head out. Second to last session while you're still an in-house patient."

"Good. I can't wait to get home."

"Now that's the spirit." Lucie wheeled her out of the room.

"I do have a question, though."

"Go for it."

"Will I need a wheelchair at home, or crutches?"

"Both." Lucie grinned at the exasperated look Talia gave her. "A wheelchair until you get more used to the crutches, which I'm going to suggest that you use as much as possible to start out."

"And then what?"

"Later we'll see about moving up to a cane when you're stronger and have your permanent prosthesis."

Talia stopped her from going into the therapy room. "Honestly, Lucie, are you sure I'll be able to walk on my own again?"

Lucie touched her shoulder and gave her a gentle squeeze. "That's our goal. And I intend to keep you focused on it. Got it?"

"Sure." Talia quieted as Lucie wheeled her into the therapy room so they could begin.

HER CELL PHONE rang, and in an attempt to answer it, Kelly nearly dropped the groceries she was carrying. Using her knee, she balanced the bag precariously against the door and flipped the phone open. Talia's name and number appeared on the screen.

"Hey, baby. How was physical therapy?" Kelly got hold of her bags, unlocked the door, and stepped inside, cradling the phone against her ear.

"So-so. Any chance I'll see you later?"

"Promise to do my best on that one. I need to get the groceries put away, then I've got an ACLS class to teach and I won't get done with that until around 9 tonight."

"You're busier on your day off than you are at work."

"Sometimes." Kelly chuckled. "How 'bout if I come by the hospital tomorrow evening?"

No hesitation in Talia's voice. "Sounds perfect."

"Great." Kelly ended the call and slid the phone into her pocket.

Marina strolled in the kitchen and greeted Kelly with a kiss on the cheek, then helped her put some of the groceries away. "I took a phone message for you. Jimmy called to remind you that there's mandatory training tomorrow."

"Damn."

"You have things to do?"

"Yeah. Ginger has a vet appointment in the morning, I have to do the second half of the ACLS class in the afternoon and now I've got training. I was going to visit Talia and I have to cancel."

"I'd offer to take Ginger to the vet for you, but I'm supposed to get my yearly blood test at 9am. I could reschedule it."

"No way. This is the third rescheduled date, Ma. You get your test done. I'll have to call Talia."

"It's just one night. I'm sure she'll understand."

"Hope so." Kelly finished putting groceries away and called Talia.

"That was fast," Talia said.

Her voice was cheerful, and it made Kelly feel like a jerk. "Hey, I just got reminded of mandatory training at the fire station tonight. I'm sorry, but I can't come over after all." Kelly didn't hear anything and at first thought she'd lost the connection. "Talia? You there?"

"Yeah. I'm here." Talia's voice was flat now, and Kelly knew she'd hurt her feelings.

"Look, I promise to make it up to you. I have to work tomorrow, but I'm off on Thursday. I'll bring coffee and bagels first thing in the morning."

"Sure. Sounds great."

"You'll be okay?"

"Yeah. Look, I gotta go. Talk to you later." Talia hung up before Kelly could say anything else.

"Damn."

"You're cursing a lot," Marina said. "You should go to confession, young lady."

"Ma, I haven't been to confession in years."

Mariana shook her finger at Kelly. "My point exactly. So, she's upset?"

"I couldn't tell if she was more hurt or pissed off there at the end of our call." Kelly glanced at the wall clock. "It's almost time to go. I'm going to shower and change, then I'll get Ginger there and back."

"Don't take this too seriously. Talia will come around," Marina said. "It's early for you two and she's going through a lot. Give her time."

"I will, but something's not right with her lately. I just don't get it."

"Maybe you should go see Father Tom. You can go to Mass with me on Saturday."

"Thanks, Mom." Kelly knew her mother was trying to be helpful, but she hadn't turned to God for so long that Kelly wasn't sure He was even there anymore. "I'll think about it. I gotta get ready."

TRAINING TOOK LONGER than expected, and by the time Kelly was in her car, it was well past 10 p.m. She flipped open her cell phone and dialed Talia's number.

"Hello?" Talia's voice was quiet, but didn't sound sleepy.

"Hi, baby." She held the phone close to her ear as if that would put her closer to Talia. "I just got done with training. Sorry I'm calling so late."

"It's okay. I understand." Talia hesitated, like she had more to say, but stayed quiet.

"Is there something wrong? You feeling all right?"

"It's nothing."

Talia didn't sound very reassuring, but Kelly didn't think she should push it. "I'll be over Thursday after my shift ends. I'll bring breakfast. Sound good?"

Talia didn't respond and Kelly wasn't sure how to take the silence on the other end of the phone. "Do you have other plans?"

"Not unless you count physical therapy as other plans."

"Perfect. I'll be there first thing and we'll enjoy coffee and bagels."

"Sure. See you then," Talia hung up before Kelly said goodbye.

SLEEP DID NOT come for Kelly during her shift the next day. She'd had ambulance duty and had only been back to the station twice in twenty-four hours. She and her partner ate between calls and gotten to bed once, only to get a call an hour later.

She entered the station house kitchen and was just pouring

coffee when alarms went off. The end of her shift was still a half-hour away. Kelly lowered her head, took a deep breath, put the coffeepot down, and ran to the ambulance.

It was close to ten a.m. before Kelly arrived home and pulled into her driveway. She shut off the car's engine and gave herself a moment to gather some energy before going into the house.

Her mother was already at work and had left a note detailing where she could find her breakfast. Food was far from Kelly's mind at that moment. She wanted sleep and that's all she aimed to get. Kelly trudged into her room, tossed her boots somewhere near her closet and fell into bed, not bothering to change her clothes.

Something was ringing in her ears. Kelly briefly wondered if it was her imagination, but imagined things didn't keep on beeping. She scrubbed at her face and tossed the blanket aside. Not quite awake, Kelly slung her legs around until her feet hit the floor and she was sitting up.

Her room was dark and the time on her alarm clock read six-fifteen. She really hoped that was p.m. and not a.m. After a trip to the bathroom, she wandered into the kitchen where her mother was busily fixing dinner. The microwave turned off, and she realized the beeping that had awakened her had been the microwave.

"Hi there, sleepyhead." Marina said. "Hungry?"

Kelly's stomach growled, and she touched her belly. "Apparently. Thanks for the blanket."

"I used to do the same thing for your father when he had a long shift. You should have eaten when you got home."

"I was too tired." Kelly ignored the admonishing look from her mother. "How was your day?"

"It's the same boring department store day in and day out. The only things newsworthy are the fights that happen during a sale." Marina put a plate in front of Kelly piled with mashed potatoes, green beans, and a helping of roast beef, covered with brown gravy. "But that was sweet of you to ask. Now eat."

"Yes, Mother." Kelly dug in, letting her body absorb the food she'd been denying it. All the while, there was something niggling at the back of her mind. It seemed important, but she couldn't recall what it was.

"How's Talia?"

"Huh?"

"How's Talia doing today? You did go see her, didn't you?"

Kelly felt a knot forming in her gut. "No."

"I figured that was why you weren't here when I left for work."

Kelly put her fork down and lowered her head. "Oh, shit. No, I was late because we had a run before the shift ended. I came straight home and went to bed. I completely forgot about Talia."

"Call her. I'm sure she'll understand."

"I hope so." Kelly pushed away from the table, her appetite now gone. She opened the cell phone and dialed Talia's number, but it went to voice mail on the first ring. "Hey it's me. I'm sorry I didn't come by this morning. We had a late call and I was so exhausted I forgot. Call me, okay?"

She closed her phone and paced in the small kitchen. Kelly made three rounds before Marina stopped her.

"Will you please finish your dinner?"

"I can't. I can't believe I forgot. Ma, how could I forget something like that?"

"Did you sleep at all during your shift?" Marina asked.

"About an hour. We barely had time to eat. It was non-stop all night. I got into my car and drove home without thinking of anything other than sleep."

"That's why you forgot. You know as well as I do that this sort of thing happens. I remember once when your father went to Grandpa Henry's house after a long shift. We'd been married for about two years, and I guess his brain forgot where we lived. Had me worried to death until your grandpa found him asleep in his old room."

"Great. Bad memory runs in the family. At least I come by it honest."

"Just keep calling her. Once you explain things, she'll come around."

Kelly dialed Talia's number and got voice mail again. That bad feeling was in the front of her mind now, and she wasn't so certain a simple explanation was going to cut it. She grabbed her car keys and headed out the door.

KELLY TOOK A deep breath before walking in to Talia's room. She was glad to find her alone. "Hey there."

Talia looked startled. "Kelly. What are you doing here?"

"You didn't answer your phone so I figured I'd come by. I'm sorry I didn't get here this morning. We were out on calls all night and, when I got home, I collapsed with exhaustion. I woke up about an hour ago."

"I understand," Talia said, but wouldn't look at her. She was staring at her hands folded on her lap.

Kelly stood at the side of the bed and put her hand over Talia's. "I'm sorry. I'd never hurt your feelings, Talia. I wanted to be here."

There were tears in her eyes, and Talia swiped her face with the back of her hand to try to hide them. "I miss you so much when you're not here. I'm being a big baby. Sorry."

"Hey, don't be sorry. That's my job," Kelly said and waited until Talia raised her head to look at her. "I broke my promise. I should have at least called you." She wiped a tear from Talia's face. "I'll do my best to make sure it doesn't happen again. Okay?"

"Sure."

"Want to watch some TV?"

"Can we just sit here for a while?"

"Of course," Kelly pulled a chair close to the bed and sat down. "When you get out of here in a couple of days, I'd like to come to your place and hang out. If that's okay. We could watch movies, talk, whatever."

"I'd like that." Talia smiled. "So, tell me about your shift."

Kelly let out a long breath. "Well, we started off on a cardiac arrest..."

Chapter
Twenty-two

TALIA PUT THE crutches under her arms and made her way to the window. It was a beautiful summer day and she was anxious to get out of the hospital. Jacob had her apartment all ready for her and "crip-proofed" as he'd called it. Another couple of days, and she'd be enjoying it with Kelly by her side. They'd be able to watch movies and cuddle on the couch.

"It's good to see you standing again."

The voice was familiar, but Talia made it a point not to turn around. "I thought you left."

"I did," Megan said. She was so close that Talia could smell her perfume. "I decided to come back and give you one last chance."

"Heh. Last chance at what? Going back to my old life?"

"No. Going back to DC with me."

Talia felt a hand on her shoulder and wanted to pull away, but didn't trust her balance enough. Instead she carefully crutched around so she was facing Megan. "I'm not going back to DC. I've made that clear, Megan. To you and to my mother. Now leave. I'm expecting some of my friends to stop by."

"Friends? Does that include Kelly McCoy?"

"As a matter of fact it does," Talia said, her voice steadier than she expected. Her heart was pounding in her chest. The look on Megan's face was very familiar, rage in her eyes, and Talia tensed for what would happen next.

"It's best you stop this little fantasy of yours now, Talia. You're not her type anyway. The sooner you both figure that out, the better."

"Better for who? You or me? And what makes you think I'm not her type?"

"Oh, please," Megan said. "She's a white woman, and you're fat and dumpy. No one is going to want you the way women like Kelly want someone. Besides, she feels sorry for you. Nothing more."

"How—you can't possibly know what she feels. Or what I feel. You never did."

Tears trickled down Talia's cheek, and Megan gently wiped them away. Her familiar touch sent an unexpected rage through Talia's body, but held herself resolute, determined not to behave the way Megan so often had.

"I know how you feel, Talia. I always have. We were good

together. We just hit a rough spot. All couples do. Now come home with me so I can take care of you."

"I don't believe you."

"I've never lied to you."

She hadn't. Talia knew that. But while Talia agreed it would be easy to go home to DC and let Megan take care of her, she knew that in a few months they'd be back to their old routine. Megan would be telling her what to do and she'd be following along. It was an easy relationship to fall in to. Part of her still loved Megan and seeing her put seeds of doubt into Talia's head about her decision to leave her.

Could they ever possibly have a good relationship? If she turned Megan away would she be alone forever? That thought troubled and terrified her at the same time.

Her heart wanted to run to Kelly. Could she dare trust her heart to Kelly? Was she hanging around because she felt sorry for her? Was it even possible for Kelly to be attracted to her? If Kelly left her, and she'd sent Megan away, would she be all alone then? Tears flowed freely now, and Talia felt her leg weaken.

"Hey, let me help you." Megan guided her to the edge of the bed. Once there, Megan sat beside Talia and pulled her close. "I love you, Talia. I want to take care of you."

"I—I can't do this right now. Please, Megan. Please understand."

"What can't you do right now?"

Talia looked over at her, thankful for the tissues nearby. She dried her face. "This is all just too much for me. Please, let me have some time, okay? I just need some time." It was all so confusing. Things felt normal—or perhaps expected and familiar—in Megan's arms. Never as safe or as exciting as with Kelly, but at least something familiar. With Kelly, it wasn't so often that Talia felt like the fat girl who couldn't find a woman in a sea of lesbians.

"Time," Megan said. "I can give you that. I'm working as much as I can remotely, but I'll have to go back to DC at some point."

"Let me get settled at my apartment and I'll call you." Talia prayed that was okay. The thought that Kelly might not want her and that Megan might leave scared the hell out of Talia. She couldn't be alone. Not now. Not when she had to start her life over again. "Please?"

"Of course. I've written the number to my hotel on this business card." She placed it on the bed table. Megan pulled her closer and gently pressed her lips to Talia's. It was the sweetest kiss they'd ever shared. Talia felt relief flood through her.

"Thanks."

"I'll be over tomorrow to make sure you're okay. We don't have to talk about anything serious." Megan kissed her on the forehead before standing up. "I just want to make sure you've got everything you need. I'll see you then."

Megan left the room and Talia buried her face in her hands and cried.

TALIA WOKE EARLY on Friday. Her physical therapy appointment was a few hours away, so she decided to call Kelly, since this was her day off. The call went directly to voice mail, indicating that Kelly's phone was turned off. She left a quick message and hung up.

Impatient to hear Kelly's voice and reassure herself that their relationship was still good, Talia dialed again. This time Kelly answered.

"Hey, Talia. What's up?"

"Nothing. Just wanted to call you." Talia could hear a lot of noise in the background. "Are you busy?"

"Yeah. I got called in last night and I'm going to have to work most of today. I'm not even sure yet how long." Kelly said something, but it was muffled.

"What? I didn't hear you."

"I'm sorry. I really can't talk now. Can I call you back later?"

Talia didn't respond at first. Kelly sounded like she didn't want to talk at all and Talia wondered if she was really working or just trying to get rid of her.

"Talia? Hon? I gotta go. Seriously, I'll call you back later."

"Okay. Bye." Talia closed her cell phone.

THE PHYSICAL THERAPY exercise room was empty of people. It reminded Talia of the hole she felt in her heart and the ache there that grew with each passing day she didn't see Kelly.

"Good afternoon, Miss Talia." Lucie said. Her perky smile was infectious.

"Hi Lucie. Thanks for moving my time to later in the day. I have more energy."

"Not a problem. We've got the place to ourselves as you can see. Want some music?"

"As long as it isn't country and depressing."

"Roll yourself over to the parallel bars." Lucie set the station to a popular rock channel. "I want you to do some walking today with your temporary prosthesis."

"Yes, boss." Talia did as instructed and twenty minutes later the prosthesis felt like it weighed a ton.

"You're doing great!" Lucie said. "One more time and we'll be done here."

Talia managed the last turn without using the bars for support. She had to grab hold at the end of her walk. "Damn. Almost made it."

"That was fantastic." Lucie helped her to the wheelchair. "I haven't seen someone as driven as you are in a long time."

"Thanks. I just want out of here and on with my life." She'd hoped that would include Kelly, but now she wasn't so sure. It was apparent that Kelly didn't have time for her. But being with Megan wasn't an option. Was it? Talia couldn't be alone. The strength she once had to leave Megan and start over was gone now. Her heart felt like it was breaking.

"Hey, you in there?"

"I'm sorry. What did you say?"

"I said that's good. It makes my news even better." Lucie said. "I talked to your doctor this morning. You're going home tomorrow."

"Really?" Talia asked.

"Call Jacob and tell him you can leave around nine. Doctor Lin said she'd get you discharged first thing. You still have to come here every day for a couple more weeks, but at least you can rest in your own home."

"Yeah, rest. Something you never get in the hospital."

Lucie wheeled her to on of the tables and helped Talia onto it. "I know. Ready for more exercises?"

"You certainly have a way of bringing down good news." Talia frowned at her. "Do I have to?"

"Just for that, you're doing double."

Talia lay back on the table and groaned.

TALIA STARED AT the clock across from her bed. Jacob was due any minute to take her home, and she hoped he was on time. She needed someone in her life to be reliable. That wasn't entirely true. Her mother could be relied upon to tell Talia about every thing that was conceivably wrong with her body, personality, work, attitude. Not the kind of reliability she craved. Who else could she count on? Her brother. Sam would be there if not for the damn war, and her father had a business to run or he would be able to do more than offer her an occasional hug and encouragement. She thought Kelly might be an addition to her tiny group of trusted people, but it didn't look like that was to be.

She'd called Kelly seven times after finishing her physical therapy yesterday. Each time the call went to voice mail. Kelly hadn't called back. The writing was on the wall and Talia made the choice to end things before it got worse. Clearly, Kelly was too busy to give

Talia the time she was craving.

Kelly couldn't support her the way Talia needed her to. Maybe Talia was being needy and high maintenance, but she really wanted someone there with her all the time. Life before the accident had been tough, but now she didn't have a clue how things would work now. She needed someone she could rely on. And the more she thought about it, despite the misgivings, Megan was the one that fit that bill.

Talia wanted out of that damn hospital and now. She picked up her cell phone to call Jacob, but it rang before she could finish. Kelly's number. She pressed "ignore" and waited for the call to go to voicemail. A message flashed that her mailbox was full, but she didn't care. Now she wouldn't have to hear Kelly's excuse again.

The tears welled up, and she let them fall. She hadn't been aware of Jacob coming into her room, but leaned into his strong embrace when he put his arms around her.

Time passed in slow motion, and each time Talia thought she was finished she remembered Kelly's touch or her sweet kisses and started crying again.

"Sweetie, you need to tell me what happened." Jacob said into her ear. "C'mon. Tell me."

Talia accepted the tissues from him and worked to compose herself. How could she tell him? Her phone rang again and she answered it without thinking. Kelly's voice was on the other end of the line.

"Talia? You there? Please, baby, talk to me."

"Don't call me that," Talia said between sniffles. "Look, I know you've been nice to me and I sort of get why. But you don't have to do it anymore. I'm fine."

"You don't sound fine, and I don't understand."

"I think it's best if you don't come around anymore. You don't have time for me anyway, and this would be easier for us both. Thanks for everything you've done for me."

"Wait, wait. Are you breaking up with me? Talia please —"

"We were never together, but if you have to give it a name, then yes. I guess I'm breaking up with you." A frantic Jacob was making silent gestures at her to stop, but Talia waved him away. "I'm sorry."

"No, this can't be happening. Talia, I told you how much I care about you. I meant that." Talia thought she heard Kelly's voice tremble as she spoke. "You have to believe me."

"I do. Thanks, Kelly." She ended the call and shut off her phone. With shaky hands she carefully placed it in her pocket.

"What the hell did you just do?" Jacob asked.

"I stopped it before it got too far. You have to understand. I didn't want to hurt her, and I sure as hell don't want her to hurt me, so I figure it's easier this way."

"I'm going to guess that hurting her is exactly what you just did. Why would you tell her not to come around anymore? I thought there was something between you two."

"There was. But only from my end." Talia looked down at her hands as she twiddled with the tissue.

"What happened?"

Talia blew her nose. "She was just feeling sorry for me. Maybe it was the excitement of what we went through. You remember the movie *Speed?* Relationships made in dangerous circumstances never work out."

Jacob was quiet for a long time, and Talia worried he was mad at her.

"I'm sorry, Talia. I still think she's a good woman and would be a fine match for you."

"She is a good woman. Don't get me wrong. Kelly's a wonderful person, but I'm not what she wants. She's got other priorities."

Jacob hugged her. "She won't be the last one. We'll find Ms. Right. You just wait and see."

Talia leaned her head on his shoulder. She wanted to cry, but didn't have any more tears to shed.

KELLY FELT NUMB. She stared at her cell phone as if it would come to life and explain what had just happened. How could Talia break up with her before they'd even had a chance to be together? Kelly thought they were friends. Maybe more, but definitely friends. What did Talia mean that Kelly didn't have time for her? They'd only known each other a few short weeks. Twice Kelly had been late and once she didn't show up. Was that all it took?

The tears rolled down her face as Kelly struggled to understand. Talia was in her thoughts constantly every day. Kelly had been planning their date, looking forward to a chance at a relationship with her. Wanting to kiss her again, to hold Talia in her arms. How could she comprehend not seeing her anymore?

"Fuck!" Kelly hadn't meant to yell, but her outburst brought Marina in to her bedroom.

"What's wrong?"

Kelly wanted to explain, but choked on her words. She sat on the edge of her bed, the cell phone still in her hand. "She doesn't want to see me."

"That's crazy." Marina sat beside her. "Tell me what she said."

Kelly told her about their conversation. "I didn't realize I'd screwed up so badly, Ma."

"You didn't screw up. Just give her a few days and call her back.

Let her settle down, and you can try again."

"Yeah, maybe you're right," Kelly lied and rose to put the cell phone in its charger on her dresser.

"You want to finish dinner?"

"No thanks." Kelly shooed her mother off the bed. "I think I'll just sleep. Things look better in the morning, right?"

"You bet." Marina kissed her on the forehead. "You sure you're okay? If you need to talk..."

"I don't know that I can right now, Ma."

"No rush. Holler if you need me." Marina left the room.

Kelly got undressed and crawled under the covers. Ginger curled up to her side and purred. Kelly put her arm around the cat and cried.

Chapter
Twenty-three

THE STORM STARTED sometime Saturday afternoon, and by the time Kelly was ready to leave the station on Sunday morning she felt like a drowned rat. Her crew had been out all night going to houses struck by lightning and to four others at the low end of the same street that required pumping the basements. The call to top it all off was a car accident where they spent two hours trying to remove the bodies of a pair of teenage boys. After the shift from Hell she was more than ready to go home.

The rain was pouring again when Kelly reached the parking lot. She ran for her car, fumbled to get the door unlocked, then tossed her bag into the backseat. She slid behind the wheel and started the engine. Her shoulder slumped when she realized she was low on gas.

"Damn." Kelly pulled her wallet from her back pocket and looked for some cash. She didn't get any farther than opening it. The picture in the center holder was Talia. Kelly took it with her cell phone and it was a little blurry, but that didn't diminish the laughing smile on Talia's sweet face. Kelly couldn't recall exactly what'd they'd been talking about. Probably one of those nonsense conversations people have sometimes.

Talia's eyes were bright and happy and aimed at Kelly.

She touched the picture with her finger as if she could feel Talia's soft skin through the photo. Her chest constricted every time she thought of Talia. The tears always came and this time was no different.

"How did we get to this? How did this happen?"

A tear dropped onto the picture, blurring it more. Kelly swiped her tears away and put the wallet into her pocket.

"This is bullshit." She put the car into gear and pulled out of the parking lot.

The apartment building that Talia lived in was four blocks from the fire station. Kelly parked her car right in front and was in the elevator before she could talk herself out of it.

She found the paper Talia had scribbled her address on only a few weeks ago and double-checked the apartment number. The elevator stopped at the fourth floor and she went directly to apartment 449 and knocked.

The face that appeared when the door opened was not the one

Kelly expected to see. The skin was darker than Talia's, the expression more severe, and the eyes fixed on her as though Kelly were some sort of vermin. "What are you doing here?" the woman demanded.

"I came to see Talia. Is she home?"

"Of course she is, but you're not welcome here."

"Please. I need to talk to her. I'm sure if you let her know I'm —"

"Are you deaf? I said you're not welcome here. Now leave."

"Look, I don't think you've got the right to tell me that I can't see her. I want to hear that from Talia herself." Her hands balled into fists, and she felt her temper heating up. Her body was exhausted, but her mind and unfortunately her mouth were still in high gear. "Tell her I'm here."

"No. But I will tell the police you're harassing her. So unless you want to deal with them, leave."

"Who are you?"

"Megan. Talia's girlfriend. And she doesn't need you around here. Good bye." She shut the door and Kelly heard the lock click.

Stunned, she walked back to the elevator, not sure what she should do next. Wasn't Megan the ex Talia had so much trouble with?

"WHO WAS AT the door?" Talia asked as Megan returned to the living room.

"No one important. So, did you finish your exercises?"

"All done. I was thinking we could order in if you're hungry."

"No way. You'll just get junk food. I'll go to the store and get us something decent to eat."

"Okay," Talia said, though she hated any food Megan considered "decent."

"I know you don't like it, but you need to eat healthy to get better."

"Right." A wave of helplessness and fatigue made Talia realize that already she was slipping back into the easy habit of doing whatever Megan wanted. Her hand rested on the stump of her left leg. Was this how it was going to be? Permanently? Another wave, this one of chilly recognition, passed through her. Megan would never be the right woman for Talia. But could she work through it to keep from being alone? How could she know? Had she made a mistake?

"Hurry back," Talia said.

Megan flashed an odd smile and left.

Five minutes later there was a knock on the door. "Did you forget your key?" Talia called out, fumbling for her crutches. She managed to get the door open despite the balancing act.

"I never got a key," Kelly said as she stepped around Talia to come inside.

"Kelly? What are you doing here?"

"I came to see you." She shut the door and helped Talia sit down again. "I can't stand not seeing you. This is nuts."

"No, it's necessary." Talia kept as much space between them as she could. "I told you I don't want to see you anymore. We can't—"

"I don't buy it. And I don't buy that you're with Megan again. I thought you said she was mean and controlling. Why would you go back to her?"

"Because she loves me," Talia said. And it was easier than being alone. She couldn't even look at Kelly now.

"So do I."

Talia couldn't quite believe her ears, and she immediately pushed all positive responses out of her mind. "Maybe you care about me, and I know you pity me, but I don't think you could be in love with me."

Kelly knelt in front of Talia and reached up to touch her face gently. Talia felt the heat of her hand and leaned in to it.

"Please, Talia. I do love you. I don't know how to make you believe me."

"I'm sorry, Kelly." Talia didn't bother to fight back her tears. "You're going to have to back off." Kelly got to her feet, and Talia pushed herself up and slipped her arms into the crutches. "You should go. Megan'll be back in a little while. I don't think it's a good idea if she sees you here."

Talia moved toward the door. Kelly stepped in front of her before she reached it. "I don't understand what I've done. Please, tell me what it was. Let me fix this."

Talia's gaze remained on the floor. "I don't know what to tell you."

Kelly placed one finger under Talia's chin and gently urged her to look up. When she did, Kelly leaned forward and kissed her on the lips. Talia's body reacted instantly. She felt the tingle from her mouth to the center between her legs.

She let the kiss grow deeper, her tongue seeking Kelly's. She felt hot hands behind her neck, urging her forward. Talia tangled her fingers in Kelly's hair thinking only about how much she wanted her. Right there. Right now.

Kelly's hand slid to Talia's breast and Talia quickly broke away from the kiss. She was breathless and fresh tears appeared. "I can't. I can't do this, Kelly. You can't mean it."

Kelly's face went from flushed from the heat of their kiss to red with anger. "Dammit, Talia. You don't know a damn thing about me, do you? I fell in love with you the minute I saw you. Believe it or not, I'm attracted to you. I want you. I want to be with you."

"Yeah, right." Talia regretted the comment immediately when she saw the crestfallen look on Kelly's face.

"You really think so little of yourself? You seriously don't think anyone would ever want the warm and delightful person that you are?"

Talia wasn't sure if Kelly was asking the questions or stating facts Kelly'd only just realized. Talia was frozen, unsure of what to answer, when the apartment door opened and Megan rushed in.

"I thought I told you to leave," Megan said, placing the grocery bag on the floor. "You've got five seconds or I'm calling the cops."

"Don't bother," Kelly said, not taking her eyes off Talia. "I'm sorry." She left without another word.

Talia stared at the door as if it would open again and Kelly would be back.

"You're not listening to me," Megan was in front of her.

"I'm sorry."

"Me, too. Sorry I didn't call the cops the first time she came by." Megan got the grocery bag and pulled out items to put away.

"What? When was the first time?"

"About an hour ago. Before I left for the store."

Talia entered the kitchen and leaned against the edge of the sink. "The person that knocked on the door earlier was Kelly?"

"Yes. I told you about it."

"No. You told me it was no one important."

"Correct." Megan stopped what she was doing. "Talia, she's not important. You need to get as much distance as you can from her. She's only going to hurt you."

"How much distance, Megan? Yards? Miles? A city?" Talia suddenly felt unable to control her anger. Maybe Kelly really did love her? What if that was true? Their kiss had certainly felt right— better than any kiss she'd ever shared with Megan. Was staying with Megan a bad idea?

"You're being dramatic again." Megan cupped Talia's face with her hands and kissed her. The kiss was nice, but lacked any of the electricity she'd had with Kelly. "I'm going to take care of you. That's not something Kelly would ever do. Besides, you're going to need a lot of looking after for a while. When would someone like her have the time to do that? And what happens when you're recovered? Would she feel that her time as your nursemaid was over and move on? I'm sure she would."

Talia didn't say a word as Megan bustled around the kitchen to make their dinner. She continued a logical diatribe to describe all of Kelly's faults, but her words fell on deaf ears. Talia's stomach hurt, and it dawned on her that she'd made a giant mess out of everything. Without even giving herself the same evaluation she so easily gave to her insurance clients, she had unconsciously headed right back to her old empty, unsatisfactory life, leaving behind any shot of having a new one.

And a new life with Kelly was what her heart craved most.

Chapter
Twenty-four

KELLY ENTERED RUBY Fruits and took a seat in the back corner booth. She had a wine cooler in one hand and her cell phone in the other. She'd tried calling Talia six times. Once she'd actually connected, but lost the nerve to speak when Megan answered.

Instead, she hung up and called Scott. Despite the fact that it was a lesbian bar, Scott never seemed to have a problem meeting her at Ruby's. He even joked once that they should compete for the same girl and see what happened.

The thought actually crossed her mind, but Kelly would never have the courage to do something like that. Especially not now.

"Hey there, hot stuff. Come here often?" Scott said as he slid in across from her.

"Yeah, and my boyfriend will be here any minute. He's big, mean and will take your head off so you better get out of here."

"Tough guy, huh?" Scott took the bottle from her and took a big gulp. "I'll kick his ass. Damn, that's warm. How long you been sitting here?"

Kelly shrugged. "Not sure. You know I don't drink that much."

"But you could have at least had another one by now, huh." He finished the little bit left and raised two fingers to ask the bartender for more. "There you go," he said, as the bartender delivered the bottles to the table. "Now you've got something to hold in your hand for the next few hours."

"Smart ass." Kelly said, but took a sip of the fresh bottle. It tasted bitter, with an aftertaste of disappointment.

"Smart and pretty. Now tell your old buddy Scott what's going on."

As Kelly peeled the label off the new bottle, she recounted everything that had happened between her, Talia, and Megan. "She was ready to call the cops on me. I'm not so sure Talia would have stopped her so I left."

"But she did kiss you back, right?"

"Yes, but that's not the point."

"But it is," Scott said. He leaned closer to her. "She likes you. Maybe even loves you. You've just got to get her to see that."

"Gee thanks, Einstein. Now that you've told me what I already know, care to impart some actual helpful information?"

"Ouch, and she bites, too." Scott slid dramatically along the bench seat away from Kelly. "If she kissed you back, then she's still into you, but she's got that Megan bitch talking smack into her ear. You just need to talk sweetly into the other ear. She'll figure things out and come back to you."

"It's that easy?"

"Nope." He finished his bottle and ordered another one. "It's never that easy. But the payoff sure is sweet."

"It sure would be." If she could get Talia to listen to her. Maybe she could call Jacob and get his help?

"I've got an idea." He put the bottle down and stood. "See those two chicks at the pool table?"

"Yes."

"Let's go kick their asses. It'll make you feel better."

"You're not drunk enough to kick anyone's ass, Sanderson, and certainly not those two dykes."

Scott winked at her. "I don't need to be. You do."

"You're gonna get your ass handed to you."

He ignored her, rubbed his hands together and headed for the pool table. "Okay ladies, who's up for some ass kickin'?"

KELLY LEANED AGAINST the frame of the fire bay door and stared at the traffic flowing past the station. She didn't pay particular attention to any one car, but watching the flow kept her mind both busy and empty. Kelly couldn't remember feeling so unsettled and out of sorts before. She'd had few serious relationships and the one with Janine had lasted less than a year. When that one ended, she'd been glad because it was more than clear that she and Janine weren't right for each other.

Last night she'd been sure that trying to see Talia was the right thing to do. If she could be alone with her again, touch her again, then Talia would know she was for real. Today, however, Kelly didn't feel so sure and had put off calling Jacob to enlist help.

Kelly sucked in a deep breath of the warm July air. She had to settle down and get her head back where it needed to be. She couldn't afford to be off when someone else's life might depend on her.

"McCoy, you have a visitor," Jimmy yelled to her from the other side of the station.

She figured it was a salesman or the Jehovah's Witnesses. They'd been canvassing the neighborhood lately, and her fellow firefighters loved to stick each other with a tiresome sales pitch. She stopped mid-stride when she saw who it was. Jacob, looking every bit the part of a high priced lawyer in his perfectly pressed suit, carefully made his way around one of the trucks. A lump rose to her throat, and suddenly she had trouble breathing. Something must have happened to Talia.

The cranky look on Jacob's face put her fears at ease at once, but also made Kelly want to back away. He was pissed and stalking toward Kelly until the wall was at her back.

He said, "What the hell did you say to her?"

"Uh, hello, Jacob." Over Jacob's shoulder, Kelly saw Scott hurrying toward them, a concerned expression on his face. She waved him off, but he lingered near the pump truck, looking as though he was worried that Jacob was going to hit her. Kelly wasn't so sure she didn't deserve it.

"Just tell me what you said, Kelly."

"Let's go outside with this." Kelly led him to a more private area around the side of the building. "I don't know."

"What don't you know?"

"I don't know what I said to her." Kelly took a deep breath and waited for Jacob to speak. When he was silent, she continued. "Two weeks ago I had a seriously bad work night, and I forgot to call her back. She left a ton of messages on my voicemail. When I did call her the next day she told me it's been fun, don't come back, thanks, and goodbye."

Jacob folded his arms across his chest. The look on his face was less severe, but Kelly didn't think he believed her. "That's not exactly what she said."

"Really? I hate to tell you, but that's it in a nutshell. Bottom line is she doesn't want me around. I don't know why. I just know that it hurts like hell." Kelly scrubbed her face with one hand. "If you came here to lash out at me, go ahead. I probably deserve it."

"She said you came to her apartment the other day."

"I did."

"And that you told her you love her."

Kelly looked at the ground. "Yes. And I do love her."

"I sort of figured that, but Talia said you didn't feel the same way about her that she feels about you. She says you don't have time for her. She has this delusion you're only saying that to get back together."

"That's ridiculous." Kelly said. "I care about her. I want to get to know her better. How could she think that? I'd never have said I loved her if I didn't mean it."

"I don't doubt that. That damn Megan stepped back into her life, and now I can barely get a word alone with Talia. That hag is always there."

"She's a real bitch. Why is Talia with her? And what's the story with this Megan chick anyway? Talia never told me much about her other than they broke up after being together a long time. She sounded happy to be rid of her."

"Megan hooked up with Talia after she got home from college. They were together for ten years. Ten years of Talia's life when I didn't have much contact with her."

"I thought you and Talia were best friends?"

"We are. Always have been, but Megan didn't like Talia being close to someone else. She's a controlling, overbearing bitch. But Talia and I kept up with each other through emails and birthday, Valentine's Day, and Christmas cards. It was hard to see her. She just did whatever Megan wanted. Megan had her convinced no one else would ever want her.

"But Colette was elated. If Talia had to be gay, she was glad she'd picked someone like Megan."

"So Mrs. Stoddard is okay with the gay part as long as it's Megan?" Kelly had a hard time believing that. "What's so special about Megan? Sounds to me like she doesn't even like Talia and she treated her like shit."

"She did. But I think part of Talia still cares about her and believe me, Megan Brugge is a very sweet talker. She was Talia's first real love and maybe Megan loved her too. Or loves her. I don't know.

"You don't beat up on someone you love."

"Megan is the Mistress of Manipulation. I honestly never understood what she saw in Talia. I mean, Talia just doesn't seem like the type that Megan would go for."

"You mean as in going for a big woman?"

Jacob nodded. "I love Talia and she's pretty, but she's not a beautiful woman in the physical sense."

"I think you're wrong there. I'm attracted to her. I see the beautiful woman she is," Kelly said. "Some people like big women."

"I believe you. But I think Megan just saw a chance to dominate someone and she did. And now she's back poisoning Talia again. Kelly, you've got to get to Talia. Make her talk to you."

"Well, I —"

The alarm bells rang and Kelly stiffened, then rushed into the station house with Jacob trailing behind.

The dispatcher's voice was calm. "Fully involved structure fire, West and Elm at the old Kroger Warehouse." The dispatcher continued with a list of units to respond, including Kelly's engine.

"Gotta go, Jacob. I'll call you tomorrow."

"Sure." He stepped back in time to miss being run over by Scott on his way to get his gear.

Kelly got ready and beat Scott by a few seconds into the cab. He sat across from her. Before she could connect the first strap of her air pack, he grabbed her hand. "Hey. You okay?"

"Of course. Why?"

"Because you look upset," Scott said. He let go of her hand and pointed to her face. "I know tears threatening when I see them."

"I'm fine, Scott. Let it go."

"Keep your eye on the ball, partner."

Kelly adjusted the harness for her air pack and looked out the window. Their station was just a few blocks from the warehouse, and thick black smoke already filled the sky. She had a sinking feeling in her stomach, one of those premonitions that told her the call was going to be bad. She hadn't felt that stomach-dropping sensation since the call at the Winchester Building when she'd rescued Talia. .

She thought about Talia and the last time they'd kissed. It wasn't supposed to be a kiss goodbye, but now Kelly wondered if it was exactly that.

The engine came to a quick stop and Scott jumped out of the cab. Kelly followed him, put on her breathing mask, looped her arm through the folded hose line hanging from the truck, and put her mind on the job.

Chapter
Twenty-five

TALIA PACED THE apartment, wondering if she was going to wear down the carpet with her crutches. She couldn't sit, because sitting made her leg stiff. Walking was giving her an ache in her thigh and her arms felt heavy and sore, and if she were to lie down, she'd fall asleep from boredom.

Twice today, she'd picked up her cell phone to call Kelly. Twice she'd put it back down, unable to dial the number. Megan had left a few hours earlier to take Colette to the airport. It didn't surprise Talia that Megan was the only person who could talk her mother into going home, although Megan had promised Colette that they would be following her in a few weeks. They? Did Talia want to go home?

Kelly was here. Jacob was here. Why would she want to go home to DC? A few weeks ago she'd fought the idea to the point of Jacob making sure her mother didn't enter her apartment. But now? Now she was considering it. Jacob would kill her if she returned to DC. Besides, they'd gotten even closer than ever since she'd moved to Cincinnati and she'd miss him terribly.

Moving just didn't seem like an option. Would Megan want to stay here? Did she even want Megan to stay with her?

"Dammit!" Talia slumped onto the couch and tossed the crutches to the floor. Her head was so full of conflicting thoughts that she needed a distraction. Megan wasn't due back for a while, so she turned on the television.

One of those sweet love stories staring Tom Hanks and Meg Ryan was on. She was about to change the channel when a newscaster cut in with a story about a warehouse fire.

THEY HAD BEEN working the warehouse fire for more than an hour. Kelly was getting a fresh bottle of air when Jimmy found her. "I need you on the RIT team. Old Man Scott's in rehab because his blood pressure is up."

"I told him to stop after his second bottle, but he wouldn't listen. Stubborn bastard," Kelly said. She thanked the engineer for the fresh tank. "Where do you need me, Jimmy?"

"On the east entrance. Got a guy over there now waiting to relieve the other team." Jimmy tapped her helmet a couple times. "Be careful, Munchkin."

"Yes, boss." Kelly picked up her gear and jogged to the next assignment. As part of the RIT, or Rapid Intervention Team, it would be her job to help get any firefighters out of the building if they got into trouble. She shifted a Hux Tool bar to her right hand and tapped the shoulder of the man standing at the door to let him know she was there.

She wasn't expecting to see Jason Burke turn around to greet her. "Nice. They put me on a RIT team with the weak little dyke."

"Fuck you, Burke. Just do your damn job."

"Don't worry, sweetheart. I'll take care of anyone that needs help. You just stand back and let the man do the work."

Kelly wanted to reply, but that would be useless. Burke was a complete asshole and nothing she said would make a difference.

"RIT 2," the call came over their radios.

Kelly answered, "RIT 2, go ahead."

"RIT 2, make entry. Team 4 is down."

"Copy that," she said, following Burke into the building.

They crawled on hands and knees, following the hose line that would lead them to Team 4. In the smoke and darkness, all she could see was Burke's boots in front of her. Kelly kept her hand on his left ankle so they wouldn't lose contact with one another.

The hose line stretched like a giant snake, covering fifteen yards along a hallway, then went down two flights of stairs before ending at a doorway backlit by an orange glow. Both men from Team 4 knelt at the doorway aiming the stream of water at the base of the fire.

Burke tapped the closest man on the helmet, said something Kelly couldn't quite make out and pointed to his radio. Kelly moved to Burke's side in time to hear the man reply with, "Oh, shit. I must have hit the panic button."

"Watch what the fuck you're doing," Burke said. "I don't need to be wasting time coming after your candy ass for being stupid."

"Bite me," he said.

"Gimme the hose line and report to Command," Burke told him. The firefighter nudged his partner, who gave the nozzle to Burke, who sank to his knees to continue spraying back the fire. They left and Kelly knelt behind Burke to back him up on the line. Just the motion of settling onto her knees made her realize how fatigued she was.

Kelly's radio crackled. "Command to all units! Immediate evacuation! All units, immediate evacuation!" The three distinct blasts from an air horn that followed were the universal sign that the building was no longer safe to be inside.

Kelly got up, her tank and gear unwieldy and feeling considerably heavier than it had when she'd first put it on. She raised a hand to signal Burke. He dropped the hose, scrambled up, and used a glove-clad forearm to knock her aside. She fell on her butt and slid backwards, the heavy equipment on her back turning her into a turtle that, for a moment, couldn't roll itself over. Burke kicked at her as he rushed past and headed for the stairs.

"You fucking bastard!" she screamed, but he paid no heed. With a twist of hips, she rolled over and got her hands situated to shove herself up and onto her feet.

Burke was already out of her line of sight. Fury charged her with unexpected energy, and she raced up the steps.

Jason Burke had just broken the most important rule of firefighting. Never leave your partner. He'd been suspended for the fight they'd had a few weeks ago. This time, Kelly meant to get him fired.

"Burke," she yelled, but got not response. She'd reached the top of the stairs and heard an explosion so loud that it shook her right down to her boots. Billowing smoke surrounded her, so she dropped to her knees to crawl on all fours. Where was the hoseline? Frantically she swept her hands from side to side, crawled ahead, felt some more, pausing only when the building shook again like an earthquake had hit. Why couldn't she find the hose line? Shouldn't it be right here? The dense smoke parted for a moment, and she saw flames on all sides, felt the whoooosh of air fueling the fire's rapid progress along the ceiling and walls.

But where was the hose? She forced herself forward, reaching, stretching, and her gloved hands found it, grabbed hold, but before she could make any progress along the line, she heard a ripping sound, then a giant CRACK!

Debris fell. Chunks of plaster and lathe hit her helmet and back. Oh, God, she thought, help me. Another explosion rocked her to her side. The air tank pulled her back into turtle position. Before she could roll over, a heavy weight hit her and pressed upon her chest, forcing the air from her lungs. She wanted to scream, but couldn't make any noise pass her lips. The last thing she saw were orange flames licking diabolically all around, and then everything went black.

FROM HER BEDROOM window, Talia saw thick smoke coiling up into the sky. She wasn't sure exactly where the warehouse was, but occasionally she could actually see flames. She wondered if Kelly was working.

On her nightstand, she saw the folded-up schedule that Kelly had given her. It felt like months ago, when in fact it had only been a few weeks ago that Kelly was explaining how it worked.

Talia scanned the schedule and saw a "B" on today's date. That meant Kelly was working and she was probably at the big fire.

"Please be safe," Talia said aloud.

"Who are you talking to?" Megan asked from the living room.

Talia moved from the window and joined her. "No one. Just talking to myself."

"Were you watching the fire?"

"Yes. It's so awful. I hope no one gets hurt."

Megan said, "I think that building is abandoned. No one works there anymore. At least that's what the news said."

"Yeah, but the firefighters are all there. One of them could get hurt." Like Kelly.

"They won't get hurt. Besides, I don't see why they don't just let it burn down. I just drove past there a little while ago, and it's an old eyesore that'd be better off leveled."

"They can't just let it burn. Something else might catch fire."

"But having to call out the fire department only costs the taxpayer, and the whole big production is a pain in the ass. Traffic was so backed up I didn't think I'd ever get back. I miss the DC Metro. Why the hell doesn't this city have a subway?"

"It does. They just never finished it."

"Hillbillies." Megan got comfortable on the couch. "Perfect reason for you to move back to DC. It's so much easier to get around. You don't need a car. Especially from my new house in Dupont Circle."

Talia was surprised. "You bought a house? When?"

"About four months ago. So, you have perfect timing." Talia lowered herself carefully to sit next to Megan who placed her hand on Talia's stump. The moment her hand felt the rounded end of the leg, Megan pulled back. "It's a two-story house, but it won't take you that long to go up and down steps. And it's close to the bookstore and the Metro. You'll love it."

"I don't know, Megan." Talia felt uncomfortable about the way Megan squeamishly pulled away whenever her hand, or arm, or body was close to Talia's stump. "I don't know that I want to go back."

"I thought we went over this. You can't stay in this backwater city."

"It's not backwater. They've got one of the best trauma hospitals in the country. They saved my life."

"Yes, but not your leg," Megan did not bother to hide her disgust.

"So what? I don't need a leg to live." Talia stood and did her best to balance on her good leg. "See?"

"Stop that. Use your crutches before you fall. What's your problem?"

"I think you are, Megan."

"What?" Megan stood as well. "What the hell are you saying?"

What was she saying? Megan always wanted her to do things one way, but Talia usually wanted to go another direction. This old struggle, so useless and familiar, was part of what broke them up the last time, and nothing had changed since. Already they were fighting. In a flash of insight, Talia realized that Megan was kidding herself. She didn't want to be with a woman who had lost her leg. Or with Talia for that matter. Talia wasn't quite sure what Megan wanted — Megan didn't even seem to know — but it was clear now that the two of them were slipping back into old patterns that wouldn't take either of them anywhere good.

A flash of color on the TV caught Talia's eye, and she glanced at video of the fire in her neighborhood. The newscaster's voice sounded excited and Talia focused on the television. "Can you confirm that Sheryl?" the anchor said. "You say one firefighter is injured and another one is missing?"

Talia grabbed the remote and turned up the volume, her attention now fully on the TV.

"Talia, I'm talking to you," Megan said.

"Shh!" Talia turned the volume up louder.

A female reporter standing near a fire engine spoke into a microphone. "Yes. At least one injured firefighter is being taken to UC Hospital. There is still one firefighter, a woman from what I have gathered, still unaccounted for inside the burning building. I believe there was a floor collapse..."

Talia didn't hear anything else. All she could think of was Kelly. What if she was the one injured? Or worse — what if she was the one trapped in the fire? "I think I'm going to be sick."

"What?"

"Oh, God. I have to get to the hospital."

"What for? What are you talking about?"

Talia turned off the television, but didn't stop staring at it. "I have to get to the hospital. I need to know if Kelly's okay."

"Kelly? Kelly the firefighter?" Megan grabbed Talia's arm and turned her so they were facing each other. "That stupid little dyke who's been chasing you? What has this got to do with her?"

"Are you deaf?" Talia pointed at the TV. "She could be the one hurt — or missing. I have to find out. Take me to the hospital. I'm shaking too much to drive."

"No. You don't need to go to the hospital. You don't need to have anything to do with that woman."

"Look, Megan, you don't get a say in what I can or can't do."

"You can stop this nonsense right now. You're packing, and we're leaving for DC tomorrow."

"Get out."

"Talia—"

"Get the hell out and don't come back."

"You can't be serious."

"I've never been more serious. I don't know how I managed to let you con your way back into my life, but this is it. I'm done. Get the hell out and don't you ever come back."

"You're going to regret this," Megan said. She collected her purse and a few other items as she went for the door. "I will be back."

"Yeah, but I won't be here. I'm going to the hospital. You just go back to your new house and find someone to boss around there. I'm done with you." Talia found the phone and dialed Jacob's number. As she waited for it to ring, she added, "I don't care what the hell you do."

Megan looked like she wanted to reply, but didn't. She left as Jacob answered his phone.

Chapter
Twenty-six

EXCEPT FOR THE tiny lights in her mask, darkness surrounded Kelly. She panted, sucked in clean air, and wondered what she had left in her air bottle. She needed to check. How long had she been out? She tried to sit up, but something heavy pressed against her chest and pinned her left arm to the ground.

Her ears rang, and it hurt like hell to take a deep breath. Broken ribs maybe? Pnuemothorax? Hemothorax? Broken arm too? Her mind ran through a list of possible injuries. She could move her legs, so only her upper body was pinned.

Had there been an explosion? She didn't remember hearing anything other than the air horn. Three blasts. Emergency evacuation of the building. Burke disappearing into the smoke.

That son-of-a-bitch. He left her to save his own ass. He purposely knocked her over to leave her in a compromised position. It was an act unheard of in the firefighting community. You never leave your partner. Especially if you're ordered to evacuate the building.

Now Kelly lay trapped by what she could only assume was part of the ceiling. She remembered seeing a flash of fire above her head, but didn't see it now. At least she wasn't going to burn up. Yet.

She pushed with her free hand, but couldn't move whatever was on top of her.

The noise she heard grew louder, a shrill sound more than a ringing one. It took her a moment to figure out it was her PASS alarm, which went off any time a firefighter was still for more than a few minutes. Hers was shrieking loudly, but there would be no one to hear it.

All the firefighters were evacuating the building when she went down. By now everyone would be out. Everyone except her.

JACOB PULLED HIS car to the emergency room entrance and stopped. "Go on. I'll park and join you inside."

"Thanks." Talia managed to get out of the car and crutch in to the emergency room. The place was crowded with people. One old man in dirty clothes coughed into a tan-colored hankie. Talia suspected it used to be a white hankie. She moved past him to the reception desk.

"Can I help you?" The young man, whose name tag read Dan, looked bored.

"Yes. I came to see if my friend was brought in yet—a firefighter who got hurt at the warehouse fire."

Dan's bored face changed to one of interest. "Yeah. They came in by squad about ten minutes ago." He checked his clipboard. "Pod A. I'll buzz you back there."

"Thanks." Talia had a little trouble with the door until the filthy old man came to her aid.

"Let me get that fer ya." He coughed again.

"Thanks," Talia said. She made her way into the emergency room. She had no idea what a pod was and just headed toward a group of firefighters standing by a bed.

She had to dodge three stretchers and one wheelchair to get there. When she did, two men parted to let her through. She was disappointed to find a man on the examination table, complaining to one of the other firefighters.

"I have to get back, dammit. I'm fine!"

"No, you're not." The stocky, older firefighter arguing with the patient held his arm, trying to make sure the injured man didn't leave. "Sit still. The captain sent in a RIT team to find her."

"Find who?" Talia asked from the foot of the exam table, almost afraid to know. "Kelly McCoy? Please, I need to know."

The injured fireman was Scott and he looked like he wanted to cry. "Hey, Talia."

"Is Kelly okay?"

"I don't know, dammit. I wasn't with her. I was stuck in rehab. We heard the call to evacuate the building. Kelly's the only one not accounted for—"

The man standing beside Scott interrupted him. "We sent a team to find her. She'll be okay."

"Find her?" Talia asked, feeling the panic start at the back of her throat. "What do you mean 'find her'?"

"Burke was the last one with her. She was on RIT with him." Jimmy said.

"RIT? What's that?"

"Rapid Intervention Team. They go in when another team needs help."

"You've got to find her," Talia said.

"We will," Jimmy turned to Scott. "I'll check in with Command. C'mon, guys," he said to the other two firefighters. "Let's give Scott some air. Ma'am, you're welcome to stay here if you'd like."

"Thanks," she said. "I appreciate that."

She and Scott were silent after Jimmy walked away. Talia jumped when her phone rang. "Hello?"

"Talia, where are you?"

"Mother? I thought you were flying home."

"I was. Megan came to get me. She says you've rushed off to the hospital after that woman. Is that true? Are you at the hospital?"

"Yes. And I don't have time to talk to you. Please don't call me until I find out what's happened. I want to keep the line clear." She hung up.

KELLY WAS EXHAUSTED. She'd given up trying to move the debris that held her down. For the last few minutes, she'd been systematically searching for her radio, which had been in her right breast pocket but was now only God knew where. She tried to move her body to extend her arm, but that wasn't happening. Breathing was getting harder and the indicator light in her mask reminded her that she'd soon run out of air.

The PASS alarm was still going off, and it was close to deafening her. She didn't want to touch it in case they got close enough to hear it.

And they would. At least Scott and Jimmy would. She could almost imagine them being like those movie heroes who break the rules and risk everything to find their friend. If this was a movie, she'd be the love interest for both of them and that made her laugh. Maybe she'd already run out of air and was sucking in carbon dioxide now. Her thoughts were all jumbled and nothing made any sense.

She closed her fingers around a curly cord. The radio? She tugged on it and felt something heavy at the other end. Kelly kept pulling on it until the unit rested against her side. She fumbled to find the top of the radio and pressed the emergency button in the center.

It wouldn't make any noise and with the PASS going off she couldn't tell if the radio was on or not, but this was all she could do.

The lights in her face mask faded in and out, and Kelly wondered just how much time she had left.

TALIA WAITED IN the emergency room, staring at the floor, and unable to look up at Scott. She felt guilty. For what? For not believing that Kelly loved her? For not following her heart?

Scott's firefighter friends had left the emergency room. Jimmy had returned to the warehouse fire. Jacob waited with them for a while, then left to find something for Scott and Talia to eat. Now she sat alone, fear coursing through her veins.

"Hey, she's pretty damn tough, ya know?" Scott said.

Talia finally met his gaze. He looked like he was trying to convince himself as much as her. "I know. Tough little New Yorker."

"Heh. You don't know the half of it," he said. "Did she ever tell you about the pile? About what she did down there?"

"She said she worked on it for a few weeks. Told me a story about a counselor she met. That was about it. It was painful for her to talk about."

"It is. But what you should know is that she was there when it happened. Her company was one of the first rescue units on the scene. And she was one of the last to leave."

It didn't surprise Talia. "I have a feeling there's a lot about her I don't know."

"She was trapped temporarily in one of the buildings damaged when the towers fell. She and a couple other guys. So trust me, she found her way out then. She'll find it now."

"Thanks, Scott. I hope you're right."

"I'm always right. You'll see."

WHAT WAS THE name of that movie, Kelly wondered? The one about the firefighter who got trapped in a building and died. Now that was a nice thought. She knew it could be true, too. Would Talia be at her funeral? Would someone even tell her Kelly died?

Kelly's father died in the line of duty. Guess she was following in his footsteps in more ways than one. She'd survived the collapse of the buildings at Ground Zero in New York. She'd had other close calls at fires, and she'd survived more than any sane person ever should go through. Was a roof collapse going to be her downfall?

Might have been easier to take if she'd had more time with Talia. Kelly wanted one more chance to hold her close, feel her kiss, enjoy the softness of her skin. Why hadn't she been able to convince Talia that she was completely in love with her? Kelly was more than certain she'd found her soulmate, as corny as that sounded. And now she'd never get to tell her how she felt, share a morning cup of coffee in their home, cuddle through a long cold evening, or make love. She didn't want to be greedy, but if she could hear Talia's voice one more time...

Damn. This was all too crazy. And each time she tried to focus her thoughts, they just ran off on courses she couldn't control.

Breathing was so painful Kelly wanted to stop. The lights were out in her mask, and now she was breathing whatever bad air surrounded her. Everything seemed fuzzy. Her body jolted a few times, and it took a while to understand that she was coughing. Not enough oxygen was reaching her lungs. The pain was so intense now that she felt like one more fit would be her last.

Then a light shone in her eyes, blinding her. Was this it? Was she on her way to see her dad again? But the light moved up, down, sideways, until it steadied on her face. Behind it, she saw movement. She couldn't hear anything, but felt the weight lifted off her chest.

Then the light went out.

Chapter
Twenty-seven

THE EMERGENCY ROOM had quieted down, and they'd moved Scott into an alcove for continued monitoring. Jacob returned with sandwiches and coffee for Talia, Scott, and himself, but no one was hungry enough to eat more than a few bites. Talia hadn't eaten for hours but knew she needed to choke something down. The sandwich and coffee left a bitter taste in her mouth, and she set them aside unfinished.

"This is torture," Scott said.

Jacob glanced at his watch and released a deep breath. "It's been an hour. Why don't they tell us anything?"

Talia had ceased crying, and now all she could think about were the missed opportunities, the overlooked chances to be close to Kelly, to let her know how she felt. What had gotten in the way? Pride? Fear? Talia shook her head. More like stupidity. Why couldn't I have enjoyed what I had while I had it? Instead, I sent her away, and now she's probably lying in some debris pile without some nice paramedic to crawl in and hold her hand, keep her from crying, and be there through it all. I've failed, Talia thought. And now she's probably dead.

She pressed a fist to her lips, choking back her emotions.

Scott said, "Hey, come on, Talia. Don't give up. They probably already got her out. It takes a while to get news especially if it's good news. If it was bad news we'd have heard by—"

"We got her!" a voice called out. Jimmy came running toward them, one hand holding a radio, the other a cell phone pressed to his ear. "They just pulled her out. She's on her way."

With difficulty, Talia stood and balanced on her crutches. "Is she okay?"

"She's hurt, but she's alive."

KELLY WOKE TO the sound of something beeping and not the shrill PASS noise she remembered hearing. These tones were steady and distant. Breathing still hurt and her left arm was too heavy and painful to lift. Was she in the hospital? She could hear people talking in muffled voices. Her eyes couldn't focus on anything.

Am I out? Am I safe?

She wanted to move her head to look around, but that caused a pounding sensation that made her want to puke. She didn't think nausea would be so strong if she were dead, so she added concussion to her list of injuries.

Kelly closed her eyes and tried to remember what happened. She'd fallen and something had pinned her down. The pain with breathing was the worst part. And the sound of the PASS alarm going off. She hoped she'd never hear that awful sound again.

"Hey?" Kelly heard her mother's voice. "I'm here, sweetie. You're going to be okay."

"Ma," Kelly said, despite the dryness of her throat. "What?" She opened her eyes and saw blurry shapes and sharp angles.

"Not now." Her mother drew close enough that Kelly could see her concerned face.

"Water? Please?"

"Sure." Marina got a cup of water and a straw, holding the straw close enough for Kelly to take a few sips. "Not too much. Nurse's orders."

"Thanks. Ribs broken?"

"Shhh." Marina smoothed back the hair on Kelly's forehead. "Yes, broken ribs, broken arm and a concussion. Which all add up to you needing a lot of rest, young lady."

Kelly wanted to ask more questions, but felt her strength waning.

"Hey, Kel," Scott said. He leaned over the bed so she could see him. "Good to see you awake. Had me worried for a minute."

"I bet. You okay?" Kelly said.

Scott gently touched her hand. "I got out just fine."

"Good. Burke? He got out?"

"Yeah," Scott said and kissed her on the forehead. "We'll talk about that later. The nurse said they'll be taking you to a room shortly."

"Wonderful," Marina said. "Then we can get out of this noisy emergency room."

"Exactly." Scott moved to Marina's side. "But you and I are gonna get a bite to eat while they settle Kelly in. I've got the room number and you don't get a choice."

Marina crossed her arms and gave Scott a stern, motherly look. "I'm not going anywhere."

"Ma, go eat. I'm fine."

"You're not helping," Marina said. "What if something happens?"

"They have my cell number." Scott turned Marina toward the door. "We'll see you in about a half hour, Kel."

Kelly gave them a weak smile, and heard her mother's protests fade as they went off toward the cafeteria. She closed her eyes and let her tired, sore body shut down.

It could have been minutes or hours later when she woke up. Either way, Kelly didn't feel rested. Someone was talking, but it took her a while to figure out the words and the voice. Was that Talia? It couldn't be. How would she know Kelly was in the hospital?

Kelly opened her eyes and blinked to focus on the tear-streaked face of the woman who meant so much to her. "Don't cry. I'm fine."

"You don't look fine." Talia sniffled and wiped at her eyes with a tissue.

"How bad do I look?"

"It's hard to tell with all the bandages." Talia touched Kelly's forehead with her fingertips. "You have bruises and cuts..." She choked on a sob.

"It doesn't feel as bad as all that." Kelly wasn't sure if she could lift her good arm, so she resisted the urge to take hold of Talia's shaking hand. "How did you know I was here?"

"I saw the fire on the news. When they said a firefighter got hurt I called Jacob and made him bring me here. I've been waiting with Scott forever." She balanced on the crutches, not caring at all that her bad leg was pounding with pain and that it was hard to stand.

"You look like an old pro on those crutches. How are you feeling?"

The tears coursed down Talia's face. "Kelly," she choked out, "I feel so bad about what I said to you. I was so scared it'd be the last thing we ever said to each other."

"I love you, Talia." Kelly opened her hand, reassured when she felt Talia's grip. "I'm glad you're here."

"Me, too." She kissed Kelly's palm. "I was so damn scared." Talia kissed her on the mouth, then leaned back. "I love you, too."

"Then why the hell aren't we together?"

"We will be. I promise you, we are."

"Good." Kelly grinned and winced from a pain that shot through her jaw. Tears welled in her eyes, stinging the cuts on her face as they fell.

"Shh." Talia held Kelly's hand and placed soft kisses on her forehead. "It's okay. I'm here now. You're safe. You just get some rest."

"Be here when I wake up?"

"No place I'd rather be."

TALIA HAD TO leave Kelly's room when visitor hours ended at 8 p.m. and she called Jacob to come get her. He waited for her at the hospital entrance and helped her into his car.

"How's she doing?" he asked.

"She slept most of the time. Her mom and her work partner Scott left about a half hour ago. Jacob, she looks so bad. I just wanted to put my arms around her and hold her all night long."

"Then why are you in my car? Go back up there."

"I got kicked out. They wouldn't allow anyone to stay—said she needed uninterrupted rest. She looks so small and fragile in that big hospital bed. Her face is a mess of cuts and bruises. She's got more marks on her stomach and chest."

"She's strong, Talia. Incredibly strong. She'll get through this with flying colors."

"I hope so. I don't know what I'd do—"

"Don't go there. So, how'd it go? As far as you two are concerned, I mean."

"Better than I expected." Talia turned in her seat to face her friend. "She told me she loves me."

"And?"

"And I told her it was mutual."

"It's about damn time," Jacob said with a laugh in his voice. "So, no more drama?"

"Not from us. I should have trusted her. I never should have pushed Kelly away. I'll never do that again."

"Good. You never should have listened to your mother. Honey, you've got to learn to tune her out."

"I know, but it's so hard. Especially when she's right there, day and night, ready to pounce on every mistake I've ever made."

"Then you need to have it out with her." Jacob held up his hand to stop her protests. "Yes, you can. You just go right up to her and tell her 'it's my life and let me live it.' Let her have it."

"I've tried, but the second I think I've got the courage she somehow gets the best of me, and I let her walk all over me again. I can't change overnight, Jacob."

"The hell you say. You can and you will." He gave her hand a quick squeeze. "I'll even go with you if you'd like me to."

"That's very sweet, but if I'm going to do this I need to do it alone. Besides, she'll just get mad if you're there."

"It's your apartment. You can have anyone there you want."

"I know."

Jacob smiled at her. "I think you'll do just fine."

"Hope so."

Jacob dropped her off at the elevator in the apartment complex parking garage. With trepidation, Talia made her way up to her place. She wasn't even inside her home for ten seconds before Colette went on the attack.

"Why did you hang up on me? I've been worried sick. Why did you turn off your phone?"

Talia made her way to the living room and got comfortable on the couch. "Which question do you want me to answer first?"

"Cut the sarcasm, young lady. Where were you?"

"I'm thirty-six years old. I don't have to answer to you, but like I said before, I was at the hospital to see Kelly."

"Kelly? I thought you weren't seeing her anymore. Honestly, when will you listen?"

"I've been listening for way too long."

"It's too bad you refuse to learn from your mistakes. She—"

"She's not Megan, I know. I'm sorry that I didn't choose the perfect woman, but I did choose the right one for me. I never should have pushed her away."

"Megan is very upset with you. She's staying at a hotel until she can get a flight home."

"Good. I'm sorry she's upset, but Kelly could have been killed tonight. I realize now how important she is to me."

Colette settled beside her on the couch and fidgeted with the fringe on one of the throw pillows. After a moment, she said, "I'm sorry that Kelly was hurt."

Talia almost laughed because those five words sounded like they were some of the hardest her mother had ever spoken.

"I was so scared. Please, Mother. Just accept that she's in my life. If you want to be friends with Megan, fine. But stop being angry with me over Kelly."

"I'm not angry. I just don't think she's right for you." Reluctantly Colette said, "But I'll stop."

Talia waited for more. Wasn't this the part where the two of them broke down the barriers and learned to get along?

"You should rest now. It's getting late."

"Yes Mother."

Chapter
Twenty-eight

KELLY PULLED THE curtain back from her living room window for what must have been the tenth time. She'd spent three days in the hospital, another three on bed rest at her mother's insistence, and was looking forward to getting out of the house for a few hours. Any minute Talia would arrive.

It was amazing how much she'd progressed in her physical therapy. Talia had a temporary prosthetic leg and was walking with a cane. Since her car was an automatic, Talia had no trouble driving. Kelly couldn't help being anxious to see her pull into the driveway.

"She's not going to magically appear because you keep watching for her," Marina said from behind Kelly.

"She might." Kelly set the curtain back in place. "I've never been this nervous before." She adjusted the strap on her sling.

"I know." Marina kissed her on the forehead and then settled into her recliner. "She's not supposed to be here for another —"

"She's here! I'll see you later."

"What? She doesn't get to come in and say hello?"

"I'm not sixteen, Ma. And you've met her before." Kelly hurried out the front door before her mother had a chance to say more.

Talia was just rising out of the driver's seat when Kelly reached her. "Hey there," Talia said.

"Hi." Kelly stood for an awkward moment before moving close enough to give Talia a kiss. She felt like a giddy teenager.

"I guess you're ready?" Talia asked.

"Yeah. I wanted to get away from prying eyes." She pointed to the living room window where her mother was watching them. Marina waved and smiled, but never left the window. "See what I mean?"

"I like your mom."

"Me too, but can we just go now?"

"Sure. Need any help getting in?"

"Nah." Kelly opened the car door and slid into the passenger seat. Closing the door with her right arm was harder than she thought with her left arm in a sling and the seat belt proved impossible to get on.

Talia leaned in and took the belt from her. "Let me get that."

Kelly breathed in the scent of lavender and felt a weird, tingling sensation in her belly. Warm and inviting. Talia's body pressed

against hers and Kelly wished like hell that her arm wasn't broken
and they weren't in her driveway. She had a strong urge to take Talia
into her arms and...

"Good and snug." Talia's voice got her attention and Kelly
looked into her deep brown eyes.

"Uh, well, good." Kelly cleared her throat. "So, where are we
going?"

"Dinner at The Netherland Plaza, and then I thought we could
rent a movie and go back to my apartment for a while."

"Your mother —"

"Has gone home. She had some business to attend to, and I
assured her I'd be fine. I'm getting around pretty well with my
cane."

"I noticed that. Baby, I'm proud of you." Kelly rested her hand
on Talia's knee. "And I'd love to spend some time with you after
dinner."

AFTER SUPPER TALIA and Kelly spent the rest of the night on
the couch watching *Star Wars*. The evening was still young, so they
decided to watch the entire trilogy.

Half-way through the second DVD, Talia pressed pause. "Sorry.
Nature's calling."

"She can be a bitch that way. Need any help?"

"Nope." Talia managed to get to her feet and headed down the
hallway at a steady pace.

She'd been gone a few minutes when Kelly heard a thump and a
crash. "Uh oh!" Kelly ran to the bathroom, which was in the master
bedroom. "What's wrong?" She couldn't see Talia. "Where are you?"
She moved around the bed and found Talia on the floor, her left leg
partially under the bed. Her cane was out of reach, propped against
the wall.

"Why is your cane over there?"

"I hate using it in the bathroom. It's too awkward."

"So you hobble in and out of there?"

Talia grumbled and tried to get her leg under her body so she
could stand. Her hands gripped the bed, but instead of pulling
herself up, Talia pulled the comforter off and fell onto her butt.

"Need help?"

"No. I'm fine. Go back to the living room. I'll be there in a
minute."

"No." Kelly leaned against the wall next to the cane with her
good arm folded across the sling on her chest. "This is much more
fun."

"You enjoy watching a crippled woman fall on her ass?"

"No. I hate to see such a nice ass get bruised."

Talia raised an eyebrow. "You like my ass?"

"Hell, yes. But not when it's flat on the floor." Kelly knelt beside her. "It's much better when you're standing up."

Talia cracked a smile. "Fine. Help me up."

"Okay." Kelly grasped Talia's hand. "I'll try to pull you up, but I'm not much good with these cracked ribs. You get the weight on that leg."

"Right."

Kelly tugged, but Talia tugged harder and in the opposite direction, and Kelly fell forward and landed on top of her. Talia giggled.

"You think that's funny?"

"Absolutely."

"Yeah. I would too if it didn't hurt so damn much." She rolled onto her side and sat up. "I've never had cracked ribs before and I don't ever want them again."

Talia gently touched Kelly's side, but stopped when Kelly flinched. "I'm sorry I hurt you."

"It's okay." She raised her shirt to show Talia the bruises. "They're gonna be sore for a few weeks, but I'll heal."

Talia traced one of the bruises with the tip of her finger. She looked up and Kelly saw the desire in her eyes. Suddenly she felt shy. She swallowed a lump in her throat. "Talia, I—"

Talia touched two fingers to Kelly's lips. "Don't." She moved her fingers as her hand slipped behind Kelly's neck, urging her to lean down.

Kelly's lips touched Talia's, and she closed her eyes, letting the moment take her somewhere she'd only dreamed of being.

Taking a breath between kisses," Talia said, "This isn't very comfy. Can we get up? For real this time?"

"Sure."

Kelly held her hand out to steady Talia as she got her balance and stood up. "I need my cane."

Kelly handed it to her and waited for Talia to steady herself. She hadn't paid attention before, but when she and Talia stood facing one another, her line of sight was on a pair of the most inviting mounds of flesh she'd ever seen. If she took a step forward she could bury her face—

"Kelly?"

Uh-oh. Busted. "Yes?" Kelly tried to sound innocent while pulling her gaze away from Talia's chest with great effort. Oh, wow, she couldn't believe how fast she'd gotten turned on. Had it really been that long?

Talia said, "If you hand those to me, you won't have to keep holding me steady."

"Sure, sure," Kelly said. She handed her the crutches. "Here you go."

"Thanks. Shall we go back to the movie?"

"Sounds good to me." Kelly stood back so Talia could lead her out of the room, and she enjoyed the view.

"Are you looking at my butt?" Talia asked.

"Does Darth Vader wear black?"

Chapter
Twenty-nine

"THIS IS THE fourth night in a row you've been here," Talia said, watching Kelly put a DVD into the player. "Are you trying to move in?"

"We're already past the second date where I'd have the U-Haul with all my stuff in it. So for now, I guess we're just dating."

"Funny. So what is it? You only like me for my big TV?"

"You mean your flat, giant, wide screen that has surround sound and makes me feel like I'm at the movies TV?"

"Yeah. That one."

Kelly pretended to think seriously about the subject. "Yes. I like you for your TV."

"I knew it."

"But, I do have ulterior motives." Kelly settled beside Talia on the couch and reached for the remote control. "I figured I might get lucky after we watch a romantic movie or two."

"You brought musicals. What's so romantic about a musical?"

Kelly let out an exaggerated sigh. "You haven't lived. You really haven't lived."

"You didn't answer my question."

"You're going to love this." Kelly pressed her lips to Talia's and let her tongue make its way into her mouth. "I promise. You'll love it."

"I believe you." She leaned into her. "I've haven't seen many musicals."

"Sad. Very, very sad." Kelly made a "tsk tsk" sound. "I can't imagine that. My mom took me to my first musical when I was four."

"What was it?"

"*Annie*. And I loved every minute of it." She broke into a very bad rendition of "Tomorrow" and had Talia laughing so hard she cried. "Hey! I'm not that bad."

"Yeah, you are." Talia held up her arms to ward off a tickle attack and leaned back to catch her breath.

"Haven't you at least watched a few on TV? *Willie Wonka*? *Chitty Chitty Bang Bang*? *Sound of Music*?"

"Never. Who comes up with those titles anyway? *Willie Wonka*? Isn't that a Johnny Depp movie?"

"Yuck!" Kelly scrunched up her face in disgust. "That's the new, misguided version. The real Willie Wonka was Gene Wilder. No way could Johnny Depp ever be as good as he was. But I've got something you'll love. It's called *Rent.*"

"How do you know I'll love it?"

"If you don't fall in love with Joanne, I'll have serious doubts about our relationship." She clicked on the TV and snuggled into Talia. "I can't see how any lesbian wouldn't fall for Tracy Thoms at first sight. Wow. If all lawyers were as hot as her I'd have to change professions."

"That so?" Talia absently ran her fingers through Kelly's hair. "What if I don't think she's hot?"

"You will," Kelly said with confidence. She adjusted her position to be able to give Talia a kiss. "But she could never compare to you, babe."

"Oh, my. She's probably a dog."

Kelly kissed her again, this time pressing against her body. The kiss went deeper and heated up. Kelly pulled back. "Compared to you, yeah. She's a dog. Why can't you believe I'm attracted to you, huh?"

"It's not something I'm used to."

"But you've been with other women. Didn't any of them tell you that? I mean, wasn't it obvious they were attracted to you?"

"My ex never said that to me. And Megan's the only woman I've ever been with."

"Then she obviously had no idea what she had." Kelly caressed Talia's face, tracing the outline of her full lips. "You're beautiful to me, baby. You're the only one I want to be with. Never forget that. Okay?"

Talia blinked back her tears. "Okay."

"Good." Kelly settled against her again. "Ready to watch the movie?"

KELLY EJECTED THE third movie of the night and untangled herself from Talia's grip to put it away. She wasn't surprised that Talia had fallen asleep. She placed *The Sound of Music* on the shelf.

"Hey, sweetie wake up."

"Five more minutes."

"No more minutes," Kelly said and kissed her on the forehead. "I need to be at training tomorrow so I need to get home."

"What kind of training are you going to do with a broken arm and ribs that haven't healed yet?"

"The kind you do at a desk while watching a lecture." Kelly leaned over Talia and kissed her. "You need help getting to your room?"

"Nope. I'm good." Talia grabbed the front of Kelly's t-shirt and pulled her close for another smooch. "Call me when you get home so I know you're safe."

"Yes, dear." Kelly winked at her and moved toward the door. "I'll call while I'm on my way so you can keep me company. How's that?"

"Perfect."

Kelly blew her a kiss and headed for the parking garage. She had her key in the ignition when she remembered her cell phone was still in Talia's apartment. "Shit." She opened the car door and went to get out, but was jerked roughly back in. A strong arm wrapped around her neck. She tried to scream, but only a squeak came out.

"Stop fighting me, dyke. You're gonna lose."

She knew the voice, but it was hard to wrap her mind around what was happening. Was he really there? How the hell could Jason Burke be in her car in the parking garage of Talia's building?

"You're going to die for what you did to me." He was so close Kelly could feel his breath on her ear.

"What—"

"You fucking got me suspended without pay and the union rep says I'll probably get fired. I'm gonna lose my house, my car, everything. All because you couldn't fucking keep up. Couldn't do your fucking job so I gotta pay for it."

Her ribs hurt because he had her at an awkward angle with her head and neck pressed back against the headrest. The grip on her throat cut of her air, and Kelly felt like she was going to pass out. She tried to hit him with the cast on her arm, but couldn't reach him.

"Stop fucking fighting me and I'll let you breathe. I don't want to kill you here, but I fucking will if I have to."

Kelly did what he told her to, and he relaxed enough so she could draw a couple of deep breaths. "What the hell are you doing? I never did anything to you, Burke."

"You got me suspended and then fucking fired." He shoved her away from him so hard that Kelly hit her head on the rear view mirror. A gun was next to her face before she even realized he had one. "You're going to do exactly what I say. Got it?"

"Yeah."

He pressed the metal barrel to her temple, and she was suddenly too scared to move. She understood that many guns had a hair trigger that could go off if she leaned the wrong way.

Dying was not on her list of things to do now. She'd lived through countless fires, through the roof collapse at the warehouse, and she couldn't believe that after all that, it was her time to die.

Burke ordered her to get out of the car. He was quick and came around the passenger door to grab her by the collar. Her head hurt where he pushed the gun's barrel into it, and she couldn't make her legs move.

"I said get the hell out!"

She wanted to be tough, to be brave, but couldn't stop herself from shaking. "I—I—if you move that thing away from my head, I'll get out of the car, okay?"

Burke hesitated and let go of her collar.

"I won't do anything. Besides, my arm and ribs are broken. It's not like I can run." Even though that's exactly what she wanted to do.

"Fine." He moved the gun away from her head. "Out."

Kelly swung her feet to the ground, rose, and nearly fell because her legs felt so weak. She held onto the car door with her right hand to keep steady. Burke pressed the gun into her side, and the pain in her ribs made Kelly want to scream. She stifled her reaction and took a deep breath.

"Elevator. Move."

"Where are we going?" she asked, but kept doing as she was told.

"We're going to visit your girlfriend."

"No fucking way." Kelly wheeled around to face him. "No. You got a beef with me, let's have it out. Talia has nothing to do with this."

Burke grabbed the front of her shirt again and lifted Kelly off her feet. In a flash, he had her pinned to a concrete wall. Kelly groaned, sure he'd broken a couple more ribs. "She's your life. I'm going to do to her what you did to me. I'm going to take away your life."

"No." Kelly tried to talk, but the pain was getting worse. Her breathing came in gasps now. "You—you can't."

"I can. Now you either fucking take me to her apartment, or I'll go to every fucking apartment in this building until I find her."

"Okay. Okay."

He let go, and Kelly slid to the ground. Her right side felt like she'd been stabbed. The bones of her ribs crunched when she moved, and she knew she was in serious trouble. A piece of bone could puncture her lung or diaphragm and that would be it. But did it really matter? If he had his way, she'd be dead before that could happen.

"Up. Let's go."

He reached for her, but Kelly shoved his hand away. She pressed her back against the wall and used it to get to her feet.

"Move it. I haven't got all night, bitch."

She took a step forward and hesitated. If she led him to Talia's apartment, she had no way of knowing what would happen. Was he just screwing with her head? Or did he intend to kill them? He was crazy, and she was terrified he meant to do exactly what he said. Kelly always trusted her instincts and right now they screamed at her to stay where she was.

"Are you fucking deaf?" Burke leaned over her, his gun close to her face again. "Get moving. Now."

"Fuck you," she said between breaths. "Fuck you. You're the stupid bastard who left his partner in a burning building. You're the asshole that picked a fight with me at a fire scene. You're just—"

Kelly saw the blow coming and ducked. Burke's fist slammed against her shoulder. She fell against the wall and tried to stay on her feet, but her legs left the ground and she landed on her back. Breathing was harder now, and she could only hold her broken arm across her chest and try to ward off the blows with the other.

But nothing happened. Kelly had closed her eyes, waiting for the inevitable and opened them, almost afraid of what she would see. The gun in her face again? Burke waiting to strangle her?

She'd been so focused on protecting herself, Kelly hadn't heard a sound. Never heard the whack of the cane when it hit Burke's head the first time or the second or the third.

But she heard the screaming now. Talia stood bellowing, balanced precariously leaning one hand on her car, the other shaking a bent cane at the prone Burke. He lay on the ground beside Kelly. He groaned once, but didn't move.

"You okay?" Talia asked, a little out of breath.

"I—sure. I think."

"You don't look okay. I'm calling 9-1-1." She pulled Kelly's phone from her pants pocket.

"I think he's going to need an ambulance more than me."

"I hope he dies." Talia said it with such fury that Kelly staggered to her feet and put an arm around her.

Talia shifted back and leaned heavily against a truck and Kelly leaned against her.

"That bastard broke into my car. He tried to choke me. Thank God I forgot my phone. I can't believe what you just did."

"I was so damn scared, baby. I thought he'd killed you."

"He was planning on it," Kelly said. "Shit, honey, he had a gun—"

"Not now. I knocked it out if his hand. It went under that car over there."

Kelly closed her eyes and tried hard to relax. "Good thinking."

Talia kissed the top of her head. "Just promise me you're okay."

"I am now." Kelly took Talia's hand in hers. "I am now."

Chapter
Thirty

THE ER DOCTOR confirmed Kelly had cracked two more ribs. If one of them had broken, it would have punctured a lung. Because of the multitude of past injuries coupled with the new ones, they admitted her to the hospital so they could monitor her overnight. Kelly had never felt so much pain, but was grateful for the reminder that she was alive.

"Are you sure she's okay?" Marina asked for the third time.

"Ma, I'm right here and I'm fine," Kelly said.

Talia took Marina's hand in hers. "Positive. She's getting a few more weeks off work, but she'll be okay."

Marina wiped the tears from her eyes. "How did he find you? How did he know where Talia lives? Why would he do this?"

"Nothing like a grilling from Mrs. McCoy." Scott joined them in Kelly's hospital room. "I might be able to help you out here."

"That son-of-a-bitch hurt my daughter," Marina said.

"The cops are outside waiting to take Kelly's statement. One of them said Burke admitted following her to the apartment building. Guess he was just waiting. He was drunk and pissed off about the union hearing he had yesterday. The union rep told him to quit before he ends up fired." Scott kissed Kelly on the forehead. "He's going to be fired outright now. Good thing your girlfriend got to him before I did."

"What did she do?" Marina asked.

Talia held up her bent cane. "I let him have it with the only weapon I had. He was hurting Kelly. What was I supposed to do?"

"You did good," Scott said.

"Thanks. I think I'll need a new cane, though."

Kelly laughed with the rest of them and paid for it in rib pain.

"Marina, I came to get you out of here for a while." Scott offered her his arm. "Care to take a walk?"

With a sigh, Marina said, "I'm always getting dragged out by the eligible bachelor. I'm telling you, we need to get you a younger woman." She kissed Kelly, hugged Talia, and let Scott lead her out of the room.

"Looks like I get to pamper you now," Talia said as she kissed Kelly's hand. "I don't mind, you know."

"I can hardly believe what happened. I keep turning it over and over in my head. If you hadn't been there—"

"Don't. I was and he didn't finish what he started. I just wish I'd hit him harder. Hard enough to cause brain damage."

"You had enough power behind that thing to knock him flat."

"Never piss me off." Talia scrunched her face at Kelly. "It ain't pretty."

"I suppose not."

"You need some rest, baby."

"Be here when I wake up?"

"Promise."

THREE WEEKS WENT by before Kelly could walk without any pain. Her ribs still hurt, but not with every breath or the intensity she'd become used to. Her arm was now in an air cast, and she was almost feeling ready to go back to work. The "vacation" as Scott called it had been nice. Talia had spent a lot of time at Kelly's keeping her company and taking care of her as much as Marina would allow.

That part had been enjoyable, but today was the first day she'd felt up to doing something on her own, and she was anxious to get out of the house. She picked up a paper bag containing some clothes and DVDs. The car keys weren't even warm in her hand before Marina stopped her.

"Where are you going, young lady? You're supposed to be resting."

"Ma, I've been resting for two weeks. I need to get out for a while."

"I thought Talia was coming over later." Marina moved to stand between Kelly and the door and crossed her arms over her chest.

"She was. I called and said I wanted to go for a drive and I'd come to her place. We're going to stay up all night watching movies." Kelly kissed Marina and stepped around her. "I'll be back tomorrow, Ma. Promise."

"Be careful please."

"Always." Kelly closed the door behind her and sucked in a breath of hot and humid air. Despite the heat, she was happy to be outside. The driver's seat of her car was not as comfortable as she wanted and when she put the seatbelt on it hit her sorest rib. Marina watched out the window with a concerned look on her face. Kelly put on a good face. If her mother noticed she was in pain, Marina would stop her from leaving.

The real reason she wanted out of the house was to have some time alone with Talia. They'd spent a lot of time together, but most of it with Marina hovering or Scott or one of the other firefighters coming over to check on Kelly. It was sweet of them to do that, but

Kelly really needed a break. She needed to be with Talia.

At Talia's place, Kelly put her new key in the lock and stepped into the apartment. "Honey, I'm home."

"Hey, baby, come over here," Talia called from the living room. "I got a letter from Sam and he sent some awesome pictures."

"Cool." Kelly joined Talia on the sofa. "Is he still in Afghanistan?"

"For the next six months, but the crazy man loves his job."

"And his little sister." She looked through a dozen pictures spread out on the coffee table. "I brought a couple of DVD's if you're up for a day of movies."

"Thought you wanted to go out and see the world? Breathe some fresh air?"

"I did that on the way over here." Kelly sat back and rested her good arm on the back of the couch. "Driving was enough of an adventure for one day. I'd just as soon sit and be still for a while."

"Done." Talia kissed her on the cheek. "Stay there and I'll get us some popcorn, soda, and start the show."

"I CAN'T BELIEVE I've been here for eight hours," Kelly said as the last movie was over. She'd slept through the final half hour and had no idea how it ended.

"You snore when you sleep." Talia laughed at the expression on Kelly's face. "Okay, it was only a few minutes, but you were cute, too."

"Oh? You like me when I'm sleeping?"

"You're adorable either way."

Talia's lips touched hers and Kelly responded, not wanting to stop. After a few moments, she pulled away breathless. "I hate to do this, but I think I have to go. I don't want Ma to be worried."

"Would it make a difference if I told you she already called? Your phone rang and I didn't want to wake you up. She suggested you stay here and sleep."

"She did?"

"Yup. You don't have to leave." Talia shifted her position until she and Kelly were facing each other. "I want you to stay."

"Are you sure?"

Talia's kiss answered her. She stopped long enough to say, "I don't know how things will go..." She glanced at her prosthetic leg.

Kelly let her hand fall to the thigh of that leg. Her fingers traced the soft skin under Talia's shorts, inching closer and closer to Talia's hip. "It'll be fine. I promise." Kelly kissed her forehead, cheek, nose, then let their lips meet again. "I have one question. Would you be more comfortable in bed?"

Talia giggled. "You have to ask?"

They walked to the bedroom. Talia sat on the edge of the bed and Kelly knelt in front of her. "You, honey, are way overdressed." She gripped the edge of Talia's shorts, slipping them off when Talia lifted up her hips. "Hmm." Kelly let her hands slide along the soft skin of Talia's legs. "Nice."

"You're giving me goose bumps."

"It's a start." Kelly removed the prosthetic leg and leaned forward to meet Talia's lips with hers, sealing their mouths together in a searing kiss. Her hands moved to Talia's panties, tugging them free and tossing them over her shoulder.

Kelly let her hand brush against the warm, moist skin at the crest of Talia's legs.

Talia moaned. "You have a soft touch."

"I know." Kelly nipped at Talia's ear and pulled her to a sitting position. She helped Talia remove her shirt and then unclasped her bra. Tossing the clothes aside carelessly, she urged Talia to lie back on the bed and settled next to her new lover. Leaning on one elbow, she gazed at her naked body. "Wow."

Kelly ran her hand gently along Talia's side, enjoying the feel of her skin. She could barely take her eyes off her. "You're beautiful."

"And you're blind."

Kelly placed a finger across Talia's lips. "Hush and take the compliment."

Talia kissed her finger. "I'm not very good at that."

"Then we'll have something to work on." Kelly placed little kisses along Talia's neck, trailing along her chest to her stomach, stopping just above her belly button. "We've got a lot to work on."

"And you've got a lot of clothes on." Talia pulled at Kelly's shirt. "If I'm naked, I think it's only fair that you be the same way."

"Whatever my baby wants," Kelly said. She moved off the bed and undressed so fast she made Talia laugh. Once her clothes were on the floor with Talia's, Kelly leapt onto the bed and leaned on her elbow again. "Ow."

"Ow?" Talia asked and touched the green and yellow bruises on Kelly's side. "You're healing fast, baby, but you still need to be careful. You haven't healed completely, you know."

"Yeah, I never was good at following doctor's orders." Kelly shifted to allow her body to rest lightly against Talia's. The feel of skin on skin was almost too much, and she shivered. She ran her fingers along Talia's belly until she came to her ample breasts and cupped one of them in her hand. She gently pressed her lips to the erect nipple.

Talia groaned and put her hands on Kelly's back, pulling her closer. "Oh, that's so nice, baby."

Kelly suckled and moved her hand to the other breast to knead it. Talia squirmed beneath her. Kelly rose up so she was completely on top of Talia, still keeping her mouth clamped to Talia's nipple.

Kelly's knee pressed against the moist area between Talia's legs. She pushed into the soft flesh and Talia moaned. Kelly moved against her rhythmically while her tongue paid loving attention to Talia's breasts.

"You—oh, this is so good."

"Glad you're enjoying it, sweetie." Kelly traced her tongue along Talia's chest, to her neck, settling her lips against her earlobe. "I love you, Talia and I'm going to take my time making love to you."

Kelly continued her kisses across Talia's face, wiping away the tears there.

"No one's ever said that to me before," Talia said. "I can't believe you even want me, Kelly."

"I do want you." Kelly cupped her hands around Talia's face. "More than I've ever wanted anyone." She kissed her and ran her fingers through Talia's thick hair. "Believe me."

"I do." Talia rubbed her hands along Kelly's muscular back, holding her close as they kissed. "Please, I want you."

"You've already got me."

Kelly explored Talia's body with her fingertips, determined to enjoy every part of her flesh and feel the moisture caused by her touch. She flicked Talia's nipple as she adjusted her position.

Kelly's first touch made only light contact with Talia's clit, which was warm and wet and easy for Kelly to massage. Her fingers worked their magic as she kept her gaze on Talia.

Talia breathed faster and squeezed the hand on her nipple. "Harder, please, baby. Harder."

Kelly pulled on the nipple and pressed into Talia's clit. Talia leaned her head back, one hand holding Kelly's, the other gripping the blanket beneath them. Kelly saw the veins of her neck as she writhed and moved beneath Kelly's relentless stroking.

"I'm getting close...so very close."

"I know." Kelly took a breast in her mouth and gave it a teasing bite.

Talia grabbed the back of Kelly's head, pushing her mouth back to the breast. "Yes, baby, yes."

"Wow, I like this. You're getting into it."

"I like—go inside me. Please, go inside me"

"I will." Kelly gave her another nip. "I promise you, sweetie. I'm going to make you feel good." Kelly switched to using her thumb against Talia's clit and slipped two fingers inside her. Talia raised her hips and Kelly went in deeper. "There?"

"Oh yes, there. Pump me, baby. Please..."

"You don't have to say please. I'll please you any way you want." Kelly pressed her lips to Talia's and pushed her fingers forward against the soft flesh. She started slow at first, bringing her fingers in and out, matching the rhythm of Talia's hips.

Kelly moved so she was between Talia's legs, braced herself on her elbow and used the strength in her arm to pump Talia hard and fast.

"Oh god, honey! I'm coming!"

Talia's voice got even louder as she screamed with her orgasm. She clamped around Kelly's fingers and wrapped her good leg around Kelly's back.

Kelly pressed her face against Talia's belly and held on to her as she finished and came down slowly. Kelly could still feel Talia pulsing against her fingers even after her breath had calmed and she'd relaxed.

Kelly shook her head in wonder. "Oh my God—that was awesome."

"I've never—never felt anything like that before. It's never been so intense." Talia put her arms around Kelly. "I love you."

"I love you, too." Kelly put her fingers against Talia's lips. She licked the wetness off them and Kelly felt her own arousal grow. "That is so hot."

"That's nothing." Talia moved to her side, playfully pushing Kelly on her back. "I'm going to love you, Kelly McCoy, in a way you'll never forget."

"Yeah? I'm all yours."

"Oh, yeah, that's right. You just made me yours, and now I'm making you mine."

Her lips found Kelly's, and she kissed her with such a passion that Kelly felt more nervous excitement than she'd ever felt before with a woman. Wet and anticipating what Talia had in mind, she writhed underneath her touch. "You're so hot, Talia. You make me feel like I'll explode."

"You ain't seen nothing yet, hon."

She'd never expected to see such a look of determination in Talia's eyes, and from the way Talia hovered over her, so focused and intent, she suddenly realized how much Talia enjoyed being in control. She wondered if Talia had ever been able to do that before.

"You're a beautiful woman, Kelly. I thank God that you're mine, and I want to show you just how much you mean to me."

Kelly couldn't reply. Talia cupped Kelly's breasts, massaging them, playing with her nipples. They kissed intensely, increasing Kelly's arousal, and she moved so that Talia could get a better grip on her. Talia's touch and her kiss nearly brought Kelly to orgasm right then.

"Easy, girl. We're not ready yet."

"Oh, baby, I'm so wet for you."

"I know." Talia dipped a finger in the center of that wetness and traced Kelly's lips, letting her taste herself.

She kissed Kelly's ribs, licking and sucking as she went. Twice Kelly winced and Talia stopped. "I'm hurting you."

"No. No, you're okay."

Talia traced the largest of the bruises, and the touch caused Kelly to flinch. "I won't hurt you, baby."

"Seriously, it's okay."

Talia didn't look reassured. "I'll be extra gentle now, okay?"

"Mm hmmm," Kelly said, but even if something did hurt, she didn't want Talia to stop touching and stroking her.

Talia worked her way down Kelly's body, using her tongue to pay special attention to her breasts and then to her abs. Kelly couldn't stop herself from panting. Her body felt hot, like some sort of incendiary device ready to go off. When Talia touched her burning hot center, Kelly let out a ragged yowl.

"Oh, yeah, hon," Talia said. "I can see you need some gentle relief here."

Kelly didn't know how she moved so effortlessly, but suddenly Talia's face was between her legs and Kelly opened herself to her. For a moment, she felt self-conscious, but then a searing pressure against her clit sent her into a place where she could no longer think.

Talia pulled away. "Now, I think I can be very gentle here." She chuckled and resumed, and her tongue's movements made Kelly stop breathing for a second.

Talia stopped again.

"Don't stop. I want you. Please…"

"Uh huh," Talia said, the sound of satisfaction in her voice "Definitely where I need to be."

HOW MUCH TIME passed after the explosive series of orgasms? Kelly didn't know. All she knew was that she'd been so utterly consumed by passion that she couldn't even imagine repeating it. But she knew they would, and the thought delighted her.

"I can't believe what you just did to me," Kelly said. "Unbelievable."

"I so know what you mean."

Talia lay on her back with Kelly wrapped tightly around her body. She'd never expected it could be like this. Kelly loved her. She was certain of that now. Her touch made her feel alive in a way that Megan never could.

Her fingers brushed through Kelly's hair. She touched her possessively, pulling her close.

Kelly whispered, "If you were a cat you'd be purring."

Talia made a growling sound. "Best I can do."

"Your best will always be enough for me, baby." Kelly lifted her head so their faces were close together. "I've never been so in love with anyone in my life, Talia Stoddard."

"And I was thinking the same thing."

"Great minds." She leaned forward to kiss her. "I'm serious. I love you."

"I have to believe you, I guess. It sounds so very crazy to me and I'll never get tired of hearing you say it. I love you, too."

"Whew." Kelly pretended to be relieved. "Glad that's cleared up."

"Yeah, same here. You make me feel like a beautiful woman."

"You are a beautiful woman," Kelly kissed her sweetly. "The most beautiful woman I've ever known."

"Suddenly I have an ego now."

"You should. And I intend to spend a lot of years stroking that ego."

"That so?" Talia said, teasing her by brushing her fingers along Kelly's erect nipple.

"Absolutely."

"So, what now?"

"That depends."

"On?"

Kelly moved her hand along Talia's body, stopping at a particularly sensitive spot. "How tired are you?"

"Uh, I think you have that backwards." Talia used her weight to roll them over so Kelly was on her back. "The question is, how tired are you?"

MORE YELLOW ROSE TITLES
You may also enjoy:

Blue Collar Lesbian Erotica
Edited by Pat Cronin and Verda Foster

Blue Collar Lesbian Erotica is a collection of stories about the average lesbian in hot, steamy encounters in not-so-average places. Santa and her elf, a tryst in an oil mechanics pit, or what nuns really do in the convent, this anthology goes outside the norm.

Several talented authors have joined together for this collection of erotica including Karin Kallmaker, Radclyffe, Ali Vali, Kate Sweeney, Verda Foster, Vada Foster, Trish Shields, Nann Dunne, Sammo, Cheri Crystal, Pat Cronin, Georgia Beers, Anne J. Kingsley, MJ Williamz, Kathy Smith, and Victoria Oldham.

ISBN 978-1-935053-01-9

A Table For Two
by Janet Albert

Ridley Kelsen is convinced she's not destined to find love. The singles scene is old and dating is terribly disappointing. Her closest friend tells her that love comes along when you least expect it and the very last thing Ridley expects when she accepts an invitation to join her friends for dinner, is that she will meet the most beautiful creature she's ever laid eyes on. Will this turn out to be yet another disappointment?

Dana De Marco moves to Philadelphia after her dreams for the future are unexpectedly shattered. Her new restaurant, Cafe De Marco is located on the city's famous South Street and has opened to rave reviews. It seems as if the pieces of her life are finally falling into place, except for one minor detail...she's unable to let go of the past.

The last thing Dana expects is that she's about to meet someone who will force her to face her demons head on. Does she have the courage to open her heart and love again?

ISBN 978-1-935053-27-9

The Sea Hawk
by Brenda Adcock

Dr. Julia Blanchard, a marine archaeologist, and her team of divers have spent almost eighteen months excavating the remains of a ship found a few miles off the coast of Georgia. Although they learn quite a bit about the nineteenth century sailing vessel, they have found nothing that would reveal the identity of the ship they have nicknamed "The Georgia Peach."

Consumed by the excavation of the mysterious ship, Julia's relationship with her partner, Amy, has deteriorated. When she forgets Amy's birthday and finds her celebrating in the arms of another woman, Julia returns alone to the Peach site. Caught in a violent storm, she finds herself separated from her boat and adrift on the vast Atlantic Ocean.

Her rescue at sea leads her on an unexpected journey into the true identity of the Peach and the captain and crew who called it their home. Her travels take her to the island of Martinique, the eastern Caribbean islands, the Louisiana German Coast and New Orleans at the close of the War of 1812.

How had the Peach come to rest in the waters off the Georgia coast? What had become of her alluring and enigmatic captain, Simone Moreau? Can love conquer everything, even time? On a voyage that lifts her spirits and eventually breaks her heart, Julia discovers the identity of the ship she had been excavating and the fate of its crew. Along the way she also discovers the true meaning of love which can be as boundless and unpredictable as the ocean itself.

ISBN 978-1-935053-10-1

OTHER YELLOW ROSE PUBLICATIONS

Janet Albert	Twenty-four Days	978-1-935053-16-3
Janet Albert	A Table for Two	978-1-935053-27-9
Sandra Barret	Lavender Secrets	978-1-932300-73-4
Georgia Beers	Thy Neighbor's Wife	1-932300-15-5
Georgia Beers	Turning the Page	978-1-932300-71-0
Carrie Carr	Destiny's Bridge	1-932300-11-2
Carrie Carr	Faith's Crossing	1-932300-12-0
Carrie Carr	Hope's Path	1-932300-40-6
Carrie Carr	Love's Journey	978-1-932300-65-9
Carrie Carr	Strength of the Heart	978-1-932300-81-9
Carrie Carr	The Way Things Should Be	978-1-932300-39-0
Carrie Carr	To Hold Forever	978-1-932300-21-5
Carrie Carr	Piperton	978-1-935053-20-0
Carrie Carr	Something to Be Thankful For	1-932300-04-X
Carrie Carr	Diving Into the Turn	978-1-932300-54-3
Cronin and Foster	Blue Collar Lesbian Erotica	978-1-935053-01-9
Pat Cronin	Souls' Rescue	978-1-935053-30-9
Anna Furtado	The Heart's Desire	1-932300-32-5
Anna Furtado	The Heart's Strength	978-1-932300-93-2
Anna Furtado	The Heart's Longing	978-1-935053-26-2
Melissa Good	Eye of the Storm	1-932300-13-9
Melissa Good	Hurricane Watch	978-1-935053-00-2
Melissa Good	Red Sky At Morning	978-1-932300-80-2
Melissa Good	Thicker Than Water	1-932300-24-4
Melissa Good	Terrors of the High Seas	1-932300-45-7
Melissa Good	Tropical Storm	978-1-932300-60-4
Melissa Good	Tropical Convergence	978-1-935053-18-7
Lori L. Lake	Different Dress	1-932300-08-2
Lori L. Lake	Ricochet In Time	1-932300-17-1
K. E. Lane	And, Playing the Role of Herself	978-1-932300-72-7
Helen Macpherson	Love's Redemption	978-1-935053-04-0
J. Y Morgan	Learning To Trust	978-1-932300-59-8
J. Y. Morgan	Download	978-1-932300-88-8
A. K. Naten	Turning Tides	978-1-932300-47-5
Lynne Norris	One Promise	978-1-932300-92-5
Paula Offutt	Butch Girls Can Fix Anything	978-1-932300-74-1
Surtees and Dunne	True Colours	978-1-932300-52-9
Surtees and Dunne	Many Roads to Travel	978-1-932300-55-0
Vicki Stevenson	Family Affairs	978-1-932300-97-0
Vicki Stevenson	Family Values	978-1-932300-89-5
Vicki Stevenson	Family Ties	978-1-935053-03-3
Vicki Stevenson	Certain Personal Matters	978-1-935053-06-4
Cate Swannell	Heart's Passage	1-932300-09-0
Cate Swannell	No Ocean Deep	1-932300-36-8

About the Author

Pat currently lives in Europe with her wife and 6 kitties. She recently retired as a career paramedic/firefighter and works in IT.

In 2008, Pat and her co-editor Verda Foster won a Goldie for Best Erotica Anthology for *Blue Collar Lesbian Erotica*. Their second anthology, *Women In Uniform: Medics and Soliers and Cops, Oh My!* is due out May 2010.

Pat's website is www.patcroninauthor.com.

VISIT US ONLINE AT
www.regalcrest.biz

At the Regal Crest Website You'll Find

- The latest news about forthcoming titles and new releases

- Our complete backlist of romance, mystery, thriller and adventure titles

- Information about your favorite authors

- Current bestsellers

Regal Crest titles are available directly from our web store, Allied Crest Editions at www.rcedirect.com, from all progressive booksellers including numerous sources online. Our distributors are Bella Distribution and Ingram.

CPSIA information can be obtained at www.ICGtesting.com
Printed in the USA
LVOW091656310512

284114LV00009B/114/P